Amy Cross is the author of more than 100 horror, paranormal, fantasy and thriller novels.

OTHER TITLES BY AMY CROSS INCLUDE

American Coven
Annie's Room
The Ash House
Asylum
B&B
The Bride of Ashbyrn House
The Camera Man
The Curse of Wetherley House
The Devil, the Witch and the Whore
Devil's Briar
The Dog
Eli's Town
The Farm
The Ghost of Molly Holt
The Ghosts of Lakeforth Hotel
The Girl Who Never Came Back
Haunted
The Haunting of Blackwych Grange
Like Stones on a Crow's Back
The Night Girl
Perfect Little Monsters & Other Stories
Stephen
The Shades
The Soul Auction
Tenderling
Ward Z

THE REVENGE OF THE MERCY BELLE

AMY CROSS

This edition
first published by Blackwych Books Ltd
United Kingdom, 2020

Copyright © 2020 Amy Cross

All rights reserved. This book is a work of fiction.
Names, characters, places, incidents and businesses are
the product of the author's imagination or are
used fictitiously. Any resemblance to actual persons,
living or dead, or to actual events or locations,
is entirely coincidental.

ISBN: 9798565395006

Also available in e-book format.

www.blackwychbooks.com

CONTENTS

PROLOGUE
page 15

CHAPTER ONE
page 17

CHAPTER TWO
page 27

CHAPTER THREE
page 37

CHAPTER FOUR
page 45

CHAPTER FIVE
page 53

CHAPTER SIX
page 61

CHAPTER SEVEN
page 69

CHAPTER EIGHT
page 77

CHAPTER NINE
page 85

CHAPTER TEN
page 93

CHAPTER ELEVEN
page 101

CHAPTER TWELVE
page 109

CHAPTER THIRTEEN
page 117

CHAPTER FOURTEEN
page 125

CHAPTER FIFTEEN
page 135

CHAPTER SIXTEEN
page 143

CHAPTER SEVENTEEN
page 151

CHAPTER EIGHTEEN
page 159

CHAPTER NINETEEN
page 167

CHAPTER TWENTY
page 175

CHAPTER TWENTY-ONE
page 185

CHAPTER TWENTY-TWO
page 193

CHAPTER TWENTY-THREE
page 201

CHAPTER TWENTY-FOUR
page 209

CHAPTER TWENTY-FIVE
page 217

CHAPTER TWENTY-SIX
page 227

CHAPTER TWENTY-SEVEN
page 235

CHAPTER TWENTY-EIGHT
page 243

CHAPTER TWENTY-NINE
page 251

CHAPTER THIRTY
page 259

EPILOGUE
page 267

THE REVENGE OF THE MERCY BELLE

PROLOGUE

IN AN ABANDONED CORNER of an abandoned cemetery in an abandoned town, an abandoned gravestone stood slightly wonky. All the gravestones in this particular cemetery were wonky, but this particular stone was wonkier than the rest; even when it had been erected, it had been done so with little care or attention. It had been put in place not because anyone really expected to ever go and pay their respects, but simply because tradition demanded that some sort of stone must be put up for a son of the town.

There wasn't even a body buried beneath the stone.

This particular stone, which had a large crack running down its middle, had in truth been abandoned long before the rest of the cemetery had been left to grow wild. Before the town was emptied, this stone was never visited; no flowers were ever placed on the ground in front of the stone, and in time, nobody even remembered the story of the man whose passing had been marked by the stone's placement. At most, a few passersby might have wondered who he was, this man who was commemorated by the most neglected stone in all of Crowford:

Johnny Eggars
December 10th 1925 to February 1st 1955
Rest in peace

CHAPTER ONE

January 5th, 1950...

ANOTHER HUGE WAVE CRASHED against side of the *James Furnham*, then another, and then yet another. This time, the lifeboat was pitched hard to starboard, and a cry rang out from its three crew-members as they were almost tipped straight into the sea.

"Over there!" Captain Manners shouted, his voice barely rising above the sound of rain crashing down all around. "Do you see the light?"

Holding on desperately to the rope that ran along the boat's side, Johnny Eggars struggled to see anything at all in the darkness. He could just about make out the waves that rose and fell all around, but a moment later he briefly spotted a faint pinprick of light in the distance. No sooner had he seen that light, however, than it dipped back down out of view, almost as if it had been lost.

"I see it!" he yelled, turning to look back toward his skipper. "There's definitely something there!"

"It must be them!" Captain Manners said as he turned the ship's wheel, sending them directly toward the spot where the light had last been spotted. "Hang on, men, we're almost there!"

"What about the sands?" Johnny shouted.

"Don't worry about the sands, you can leave them to me! I know how to avoid them!"

Over on the other side of the deck, Father Walter Warden was clinging to another rope. He'd only been volunteering to work on the lifeboats for a few weeks, and this was by far the strongest storm he'd ever encountered in his life. In fact, it was stronger than anything he'd imagined might be possible, stronger even that the worst nightmares he'd suffered in the lead-up to his first shift. He turned and looked back longingly toward the distant lights of Crowford, three or four miles away, and then he leaned down and vomited all over the rain-dashed deck.

"For pity's sake!" Captain Manners snapped

at him. "What use are you?"

"We should have waited for a few others to join us," Johnny muttered under his breath. "Another five minutes, and there'd be six of us onboard right now."

"And what good would that do?" Captain Manners yelled. "Three, six, twenty, it's all the same when -"

Suddenly the lifeboat hit something large and heavy. All three men were almost knocked off their feet. Manners was the first to recover properly, and when he looked over the side he saw a large piece of wood getting tossed about by the waves. A little further off, several more pieces of debris were scattered across the stormy sea, and Manners felt a sense of genuine dread starting to settle in the pit of his belly. He tried to tell himself that there was no need to panic, that the debris might have been churned up from the seabed or the sands by the storm, but a moment later he saw that one particularly large chunk of wood bore part of a ship's name.

The *Mercy Belle*.

"It's her," he whispered, and in that instant all hope was lost.

He watched as the wood was tossed by another wave, but already he could see that they were too late.

"It's her!" Johnny shouted, turning to look back toward the cabin. "It's the *Mercy Belle*! She's broken up!"

"Are you sure?" Captain Manners asked, even though deep down he already knew the answer.

"I'm sure," Johnny said. "It looks like she just... disintegrated in the -"

Before he could get another word out, a wave crashed against the side of the lifeboat, pitching it steeply to the starboard side. Losing his grip on the rope, Johnny careered across the deck before slamming into one of the lockers, at which point he managed to grab hold of a small railing. As he steadied himself, another wave sent icy water spraying against his face, and strong winds seemed almost to be trying to blow him away.

A little further back, Father Warden was on his knees, making the sign of the cross against his chest.

"In the name of all that's holy," Captain Manners said, as he spotted more pieces of debris on the waves, "they're gone. We were too late." He watched for a moment, before starting to turn the wheel. "We tried. There's no point risking our lives out here a moment longer, nobody could have survived this. We came for the living. We can't do anything for the dead."

The boat began to turn back toward the distant lights of Crowford. For a moment, all three men onboard were silent, each contemplating the difficult understanding that their journey has been for nothing. The *James Furnham* and its crew had saved many people over the years, but the sea sometimes managed to claim victims and every loss of life was felt keenly. The *Mercy Belle* had been a local fishing boat, and for the community of Crowford the loss of three local men would feel like a tragedy.

Johnny turned and looked back out at the debris as he thought of the three crew-members whose bodies would most likely be lost to the depths forever.

And then, suddenly, he realized that he could see a human figure clinging desperately to one of the larger pieces of wood. He stared for a moment, convinced that he must be imagining things, but a moment later he saw that the figure was moving about as it tried to keep out of the water. The sight was so shocking, so miraculous, that he scarcely dared believed it could be true.

"There's a man out there!" he yelled, filled with a sense of panic. "Captain, turn us around again! There's a man! We can save him!"

"Where?" Captain Manners shouted.

Johnny began gesticulating wildly toward the man, who was still a good way off, but Captain Manners had already begun to turn the boat back in the right direction. As more waves smashed against its side, the *James Furnham* made its way through the storm as Johnny began to prepare some ropes.

"Are you sure about this?" Father Warden asked as he struggled to make his way over, clinging to the ropes. "I don't mean to sound pessimistic, but for anyone to survive in such weather would be -"

"There!" Johnny said, pointing toward the man, who was still just about managing to hang on. "Don't you see him? He's right there!"

"Why, I..." Father Warden looked out at the waves for a moment, before grabbing a rope and starting to help. "You're right," he continued. "I don't know how, but it looks as if at least one soul might still be saved. This is truly a miracle!"

"It won't be a miracle if we don't get to him fast," Johnny pointed out. "Get more of those ropes ready. We might only get one chance at this."

"What about the sands?" Father Warden asked. "Aren't we awfully close to them?"

"Manners'll worry about that," Johnny said,

although he could feel a niggling fear in the pit of his belly. "If anyone knows this part of the coast well enough to keep us off the sands, it's him."

Already, the lifeboat was nearing the spot where the man was clinging to the piece of wood. If anything, the storm was getting stronger by the second, and the man was clearly struggling to keep from slipping into the depths, which would no doubt claim him within seconds. Even as the lifeboat edged closer and closer, the man seemed not to notice that rescue was within his grasp, until finally Captain Manners swung one of the lights around, casting a bright glow across the waves. Finally, the man turned to look at his rescuers, and he squinted as the light threatened to blind him in the stormy night. His face, battered and bloodied and almost bashed open, was barely recognizable as human.

"I don't know who that is," Johnny said as he prepared to throw the life ring. "It doesn't look like anyone from the *Mercy Belle*, but it's hard to tell for sure."

"Is that really what concerns you at this moment?" Father Warden snapped, grabbing the ring and throwing it out toward the man, but missing him by several feet. "Why don't we try to save his life *before* we start asking questions?"

"Give that to me," Johnny said, grabbing the rope and pulling the life ring back out of the water, before taking a moment to consider his aim. "You're more likely to knock the poor bastard into the water than save him."

The lifeboat was much closer now, but Johnny knew he had to pick his moment perfectly. He wouldn't get many more chances.

"You need to catch this!" he yelled at the man, whose face was now turned away from the bright lights that were blasting against him. "Do you hear me? You need to catch this, so we can get you onboard!"

He threw the life ring, and his aim was indeed much better than Warden's attempt. The life ring hit the side of the piece of debris, but the man made no attempt to grab hold of it and the ring quickly fell into the water. Frustrated, Johnny immediately began to pull it back in for another attempt.

"You need to catch it!" he shouted. "Come on, I need you to cooperate here! Grab the goddamned ring!"

"He's hurt," Father Warden pointed out. "He's bleeding, don't you see? There's blood on the side of his head."

"That doesn't mean he can't grab the damn

thing," Johnny said. "I'm throwing it now!" he called out to the man. "You need to take hold of it, so we can bring you aboard!"

He waited a moment, to see whether the man was going to respond, and then he threw the ring. Again, however, it simply hit the side of the wood and then fell helplessly into the water, while the man focused on clinging to the raft-like chunk.

"What's the hold up?" Captain Manners shouted. "Are you bringing him onboard or not?"

"He's not going to last much longer," Johnny said, as he and Father Warden watched the man for a moment. "It must be the fear. He's frozen, he's too scared to let go."

"Then what do we -"

"Hold this," Johnny continued, handing him the rope before taking starting to tie another section around his waist. "I'm not leaving a man out here to drown. If he won't help himself, then there's only one option."

"What do you mean?" Father Warden asked cautiously.

Clambering over the side of the lifeboat, with a rope attached to his waist for support, Johnny took a moment to consider whether there might be any other options.

"Wait," Father Warden said, "you can't

seriously -"

Without waiting to hear any more, Johnny jumped down into the water, crashing into the freezing waves and immediately disappearing beneath the surface.

Clinging to the railing, Father Warden watched for any sign of Johnny, but he was nowhere to be seen. Gripped by a sense of profound fear, Father Warden grabbed the rope so that he could try to haul Johnny back onboard, but a moment later he saw a figure bobbing back to the surface and immediately starting to swim over to the man on the piece of wood.

"Come on," Father Warden muttered under his breath, "you can do this."

Reaching the wood, Johnny began to climb onto its side. He took a moment to attach the rope to the other man, and then he turned and started waving frantically.

"Pull!" he yelled, as another heavy wave smashed against the side of the lifeboat. "Hurry! Get us back onboard!"

CHAPTER TWO

"WE'VE GOT ONE MAN!" Captain Manners shouted as he began to clamber down from the side of the lifeboat. "Hurry! He needs help!"

Rushing across the beach, several figures made their way toward the spot where Manners was wading ashore. Slipping on the wet pebbles, the old man dropped down to his hands and feet, and he had to be helped up by Nurse Hazel Christie as she finally got close enough.

"Where are they?" she asked frantically. "Where's the *Mercy Belle*?"

"Destroyed," Captain Manners gasped. "There's nothing left of it."

"Are you sure?"

"It happened!" he shouted angrily. "It's in

pieces out there in the storm!"

"What about -"

"We saved one man," he continued, turning to watch as Johnny and Father Warden helped the rescued figure down from the boat. "He's insensible, he seems to have taken a blow to the head. His face... there's not much left of it!"

"But the others," Hazel stammered, "what about -"

"I already told you, we saved one man!" Captain Manners snapped angrily. "There was no sign of the others! John Lund and his two crewmates are dead. We couldn't even find their bodies."

Hazel hesitated for a moment, shocked by the news, before remembering that her priority was to treat any injured men. After helping Captain Manners to sit on a block, she hurried over to the others, reaching them just as they set the rescued man down onto the ground.

"He's got a nasty cut to the head," Johnny said, barely able to get the words out as he shivered in his soaked clothes. "He hasn't spoken a word. He's alive, I can tell that, but he doesn't really respond to anything."

"Let me see," Hazel replied. "Help me get him onto his back."

Together, they rolled the man over, and then

Hazel shone her flashlight directly at his bloodied face. The man's cheeks had been smashed, and part of his scalp had been torn away. The center of his face was split, revealing the bloodied meat beneath what was left of his flesh.

"I don't recognize him," she said. "Do you know who he is?"

"There's not much left to recognize," Johnny replied. "I don't think he's from the crew, though. I can't imagine what a stranger would have been doing out there on the *Mercy Belle* at this time of night. We all know John Lund never had any time for fools. I can just about believe that he might have accidentally ended up caught in that storm, since it came on so fast, but he certainly wouldn't have had any strangers onboard. The whole thing makes absolutely no sense at all."

He watched Hazel work for a moment.

"You know," he continued, "I was the one who jumped in and saved him."

"Well done," she muttered.

"It was pretty risky," he added. "What else could I do, though? A man's life was at stake and -"

"I get it," she said through gritted teeth, "you're a real hero. Now would you mind trying to find me a dry towel?"

"Doctor Ford's here," Father Warden

pointed out, as another figure hurried over to join them on the beach.

"Out of my way!" Doctor Ford said, pushing Hazel aside as he set his case down and dropped to his knees so that he could examine the injured man. "What have you ascertained so far, woman?"

"I only just got to him," she explained. "He seems -"

"As I thought, you haven't done a damn thing," Doctor Ford said angrily, as he stood and grabbed the man's shoulders. "Okay, he's taken quite a gash to his head, so I'm going to need to get him to my surgery. Are you all ready to help carry him? That's right, get into position. We'll lift him on three. One. Two. Three!"

***

"I see the old man's bedside manner hasn't improved much," Johnny muttered under his breath a short time later, as he watched Hazel gathering a few items in the storeroom at the surgery. "What crawled up his backside and died, huh?"

"Will you please be quiet?" she hissed, turning to him. "If he hears you talking like that, he'll blow a gasket."

"Is there some unwritten rule that says all doctors have to be grumpy old bastards?" Johnny continued. He took a moment to adjust the blanket that was wrapped around his shoulders, and then he pushed some matted wet hair from across his forehead. "Frankly, I wouldn't be surprised if he ends up killing the poor sod on his table tonight. If I was the patient, I'd much rather have *you* looking after me."

"You never stop, do you?"

"I never stop *what*?"

She turned to him with a faint smile, before returning her attention to the supply cupboard and taking a few more items.

"You know, I really *did* leap into the water to save the poor guy," he explained. "I didn't think of my own safety at all. I just jumped right in."

He waited, but this time she didn't respond at all.

"So is he going to be alright?" he asked.

"He's certainly been in the wars," she replied, as she made her way to the door. "If anyone can help him, though, it's Doctor Ford. Despite what you might say about his bedside manner, he's the best doctor I've ever worked with. Come on, I can't leave you in here, not with all the medicine."

"Are you worried I might take some?"

"Get out. Come on."

Johnny did as he was told, and then he stopped in the corridor and watched as Hazel locked the door.

"About the other week," he said after a moment. "I can be a pig-headed buffoon sometimes, especially when I've had a drink. I can get a little... boisterous. I hope I didn't offend you in any way."

"Oh, how could you possibly have offended me?" she asked.

"I didn't mean to imply that you're a lady of questionable morals," he continued. "I know you're not that. I suppose I just had a couple of beers too many and -"

"A couple?"

"Several, then." He began to follow her along the corridor. "The thing is," he added, "this could all have been avoided if you'd just agreed to meet me one evening. I know that sounds a little pushy, but I'd really like to take you to the pictures some time. Or dancing. We could go dancing."

"You? Dancing?"

"I can dance."

"You can't dance."

"I *can* dance!"

"I've seen you try."

"I can dance," he said again, as they headed

into the exam room. "Is there something wrong with my dancing? No-one's ever criticized my dancing before."

"About time!" Doctor Ford snapped, as he snatched the items from Nurse Christie's hands. "Did you fall asleep in there? This man has a broken leg."

"Hey, he's awake," Johnny said, hurrying over to the table, where the man from the sea was sitting up and looking around. "My friend, what -"

"Get out of my way!" Doctor Ford hissed, pushing him aside. "Nurse, does this cretin have to be in here? When I asked you to check whether he had hypothermia, it wasn't because I was worried for his health." He cast a disgusted glance at Johnny. "I was rather hoping that something might finally shut him up."

"That seems a little uncalled for," Johnny pointed out.

"I have to go," the man on the table said, trying to climb off, only for Hazel to gently push him back down. "I can't be here."

"On the contrary," Doctor Ford said, "this is the only place for you right now. We've cleaned that wound on your head, but I'm afraid that it's going to need a couple of stitches. Then we need to look at your leg. I also want to check you for any other injuries. We don't know how long you spent out there in the elements, but I wouldn't be at all surprised if you experience complications." He poured some liquid onto a piece of cotton wool, and then he stepped closer to the man. "This will hurt," he explained, "but I'm afraid you'll just have to put up with that."

"I have to -"

Before he could finish, the man flinched as Doctor Ford began to dab at one of the wounds on his cheek.

"Everything's going to be alright," Hazel told the man, as she placed a hand on his arm. "You're safe now. We're going to take good care of you."

She paused for a moment, looking at his horrific injuries. She wanted to tell him that everything would be alright, but she couldn't quite find the words. Already, she could tell that the man's face would end up with significant scarring.

"So who *are* you?" Johnny asked as he stepped closer to the table. "What were you doing on the *Mercy Belle*? What happened out there? What happened to Captain Lund and the others?"

"There'll be time for all of that later," Hazel said firmly. "Johnny, we really need to get on with things here."

"Three men are missing, presumed drowned," Johnny continued, watching the man closely. "They were friends of mine. Good friends, actually. They were well liked in Crowford, they had families, they had lives, they -"

"Later, Johnny!" Hazel added, interrupting him.

"I just -"

"I don't know," the man on the table said, before wincing again as Doctor Ford began to put stitches in the wound on his left cheek.

"What do you mean by that?" Johnny asked. "How can you not know?"

"I mean, I don't know what happened," the man replied, his voice trembling slightly. "I don't know the answer to any of your questions."

"Then let's start with a real simple one," Johnny said. "Who are you? Are you from round here? What's your name?"

"That's what I'm trying to tell you," the man continued. "I don't remember anything from before I woke up in here just now. I don't know anything about a boat, or being rescued, or how I ended up with all these injuries." He paused for a moment, with fear in his eyes. "I don't even know my own name."

CHAPTER THREE

"I CAN TAKE IT from here," Father Warden said as he threw the last bag onto the side of the *James Furnham*, which was finally back in the boathouse. "It's been a long night, I'll lock up. You should go home and get some rest."

He waited for a reply, and then he turned to see that Captain Manners was sitting in the doorway with his head in his heads. For a moment, the old man appeared utterly broken, as if he was lost in his own world. His shoulders were rounded and hunched, and he sat silhouetted against the rain that was still crashing down outside.

"Captain Manners?" Father Warden continued, approaching him cautiously. "Are you okay?"

"We lost three men tonight," Captain Manners replied, not looking up at him. "Three good men, all with wives and children in the town. We're supposed to save people when they get into trouble at sea, Walter. They trust us to be there when they need us, and tonight we let them down."

"We can't save everyone."

"We should have saved the crew of the *Mercy Belle*."

"We did everything in our power. We even set out without enough crew, just so that we'd have a chance. We put our own lives on the line, we -"

"And is that supposed to be enough?" Captain Manners snapped, turning to him. "Are we supposed to go home and tell ourselves that even though three women were widowed tonight, even though five children lost their fathers, we did our best and therefore we can sleep soundly tonight?"

Father Warden hesitated, fully aware that anything he said might come across as insufficient.

"I thought not," Captain Manners continued, before reaching into his pocket and pulling out a silver hip flask. He unscrewed the lid and immediately took a long, much-needed swig of whiskey.

"I can tell you one thing," Father Warden said. "I can tell you that drinking isn't the answer."

"When was the last time you got drunk?"

"Never."

"Then how do you know whether it's the answer or not, eh? How do you know anything, Walter, when you've spent your entire life hidden away in one church or another?"

"I don't think that's entirely fair," Father Warden replied. "I do my best, every day, to tend to the needs of this parish. You might be right, Captain Manners, when you say that I do not know everything about your life and your work, but I should point out that you in turn do not know everything about *my* life and work. And at least I am trying to help. I volunteered to work on the lifeboat precisely because I worried that I was too hidden away. I am here to help anyone who needs it, and that includes you."

He watched as the old man took another swig of whiskey.

"Please," he continued, "let me try to -"

"Thank you for offering to lock up," Captain Manners said, getting to his feet and then unsteadily stumbling to the door. "That's much appreciated, Father Warden. It's nice to know that I can count on you."

"You've forgotten your raincoat," Father Warden replied. "You'll get -"

Stopping, he realized that he was too late. Captain Manners was already out of sight, already out there in the rain and no doubt already drenched. After briefly considering running after him, Father Warden realized that there was no real point, and that the old man only had a short walk home. He took a moment, instead, to ask the Lord to watch over everyone in Crowford over the next few days, and then he got to work making sure that all the ropes on the lifeboat were properly in place. He took pride in his volunteer work, and he wanted to be doubly sure on this occasion that Captain Manners would have no grounds to be critical come the following morning.

After a few minutes, once he was satisfied, Father Warden slipped into his own raincoat, grabbed the keys, and then made his way to the back door. He stopped and looked outside, and he saw that the rain was falling harder and faster than ever, although he fancied that the worst of the storm would soon be over. That would be a blessed relief, although as he locked the door he found himself wondering yet again why John Lund had ever considered taking the *Mercy Belle* out when everyone had known bad weather was coming.

The mistake had cost Lund his life, and the lives of two of his crewmates, and Father Warden felt certain that over the next few days he would be kept extremely busy. Already, he was making plans to visit the families of the dead, to offer them whatever help and guidance they might need. He knew that he'd be getting no sleep.

He double-checked the door, and then he turned to hurry home so that he could collect a few things.

Suddenly he saw that a figure was standing nearby, watching him from the shadows of the shelter than ran along the side of the boathouse.

"I'm sorry," Father Warden said, unable to hide the fact that he was more than a little startled, "I didn't know that anyone was..."

His voice trailed off as he realized that the figure seemed to be simply staring at him. Unable to make out any of the figure's features, Father Warden squinted slightly, and for a moment he actually considered the possibility that the 'figure' was in fact a trick of the light, a mirage in the stormy night air. After a few seconds, however, he realized that there was definitely somebody there, although this individual – whoever he might be – seemed to have nothing to say for himself.

"Can I help you?" Father Warden asked.

Again, he received no reply.

"It's late," he continued, "and this doesn't

seem much like the kind of night for being out. You'd probably be happier, and certainly drier, at home. If you're wondering about the commotion tonight, I'm afraid I can't really say anything yet, not until the families have been -"

"Where is he?" a voice asked suddenly, dark and grave in the night air.

"I'm sorry?" Father Warden replied, although he was already starting to think the he recognized that voice. He just wasn't sure where from.

"Where is he?" the voice asked again.

"I don't know who you -"

"You will give him to us," the voice continued, interrupting him yet again. "He's ours."

"You mean the man we rescued?" Father Warden hesitated. "He needed help. The poor man was badly hurt, he was clinging to debris and he required immediate medical attention."

"You have no right to interfere," the voice said firmly. "We are ready to take him."

"I'm terribly sorry," Father Warden replied cautiously, "but I'm afraid I don't quite understand. You really -"

Before he could get another word out, he saw the figure step forward. In that moment, he was able to make out a pale face staring back at him, and he realized that he recognized the face, although his first thought was that he must be imagining things.

"John?" he stammered. "John Lund? We thought..."

His voice trailed off, and his mind was racing as he tried to understand exactly what was happening. Had Lund, and perhaps the two other men, somehow survived the wreck of the *Mercy Belle* after all?

For a few seconds he felt a sense of hope rumbling in his chest, until he saw that Lund's stony expression seemed strangely lifeless. The man's eyes were sunken slightly into their sockets, and a moment later Father Warden saw that small crabs were eating through the flesh of his left cheek. The image was horrifying, and as much as he tried to tell himself that he must be imagining things, Father Warden realized finally that he was face to face with a man who appeared to be dead. A man he *knew* had just been lost in the storm, and who could not possibly have made his way ashore unaided.

"He is ours," Captain Lund groaned, his voice sounding so very stiff now as rain continued to crash down all around. "You will give him to us, or we will have our vengeance on this entire town. You have five years from this day to deliver that man, or as God is my witness the people of

Crowford will suffer. This is what the sea commands."

Father Warden opened his mouth to reply, but in that moment he saw that some kind of dark powder appeared to be dribbling from Captain Lund's lips. He realized quickly that the powder was wet sand, which seemed now to be gushing from the dead man's mouth, as if it had filled his body entirely. Mixed in with the sand, there were more crabs, along with assorted other creatures from the depths of the sea, and finally Captain Lund took a step forward and then dropped to his knees. Except, looking down, Father Warden saw that the man's legs had actually begun to crumble, as if his entire body was falling apart.

"Five years!" Captain Lund managed to gasp, as more sand tumbled from his mouth. "Five years or you all pay!"

With that, he fell forward and disintegrated, leaving nothing behind but a foul-smelling pile of sand and crabs that quickly got washed away by the rain.

Father Warden stared at the mess for a moment, his mind racing with shock, and finally he did the only thing that he really felt he *could* do at that moment.

He fainted.

CHAPTER FOUR

Five years later...

PUSHING THE PRAM ALONG Water Street, Hazel Christie smiled as she looked down at her son. Tobias was gurgling a little as he wriggled in his blankets, but he didn't seem to be quite awake just yet.

"Sorry!" Hazel gasped, as she suddenly realized that she'd almost driven the pram straight into a man coming the other way, and then she froze as she saw a familiar face staring back at her.

"And good afternoon to you, too," Johnny Eggars said with a faint smile, before looking down at the pram. "I guess this must be the little guy I've heard so much about."

"Tobias," Hazel stammered, barely able to

get the name out. She knew there was no reason to be nervous, but she'd been managing to successfully avoid Johnny for a while now and she'd hoped to do so for a little longer. "I mean, that's his name. Tobias. We named him after my grandfather."

"Congratulations," Johnny replied, peering in and taking a look at the baby. "You and Edward must be so pleased."

Hazel managed a thin, pained smile.

"You're cute, aren't you?" Johnny continued as he looked into the pram. "Such a handsome little guy. Look at that cute little face."

"A lot of people say that he looks like his father," Hazel managed to say, figuring that she had to come up with something.

"Nah," Johnny replied, stepping back and looking at her, "I don't see that." He paused, and then he shrugged. "I don't know. Maybe. It's kind of hard to tell. I think he looks a little more like you. How are you keeping, Hazel, anyway? How's motherhood treating you?"

"Fine," she said quickly, perhaps too quickly. She knew she was coming across as somewhat evasive, but she couldn't find a way to make herself relax. "I'm sorry, we're in quite a hurry today, we have a lot of errands to run. I hope you don't think that I'm rude if we keep going."

"Of course not," Johnny said, stepping back so that she could push the pram past. "It was nice to see you, though. We should catch up some time."

"You too," she murmured, but she was already disappearing into the distance and she quickly rounded the corner onto Nelson Street, leaving Johnny standing all alone.

"Yeah," he muttered, shoving his hands into his pockets as he turned and headed across the road, toward the tobacconist's shop on the far corner. "Nice to see you too. Great. Wonderful. Nice baby. I hope life's going just swimmingly for you."

The bell above the door rang as Johnny stepped into the shop, and he made his way immediately over to the counter, where Mr. Mellor already had his usual order ready.

"Having a good day there, Johnny?" the older man asked. "How's your uncle?"

"He's fine. I'll give him your best."

"You look a little down in the dumps."

"Nothing a drink won't fix," Johnny replied, quickly paying him before turning and heading to the door. "See you around. Keep up the good work."

He reached out to open the door, but then he hesitated as he spotted a card in the window. He stepped outside and took a look, and he was surprised to see that somebody was offering dance classes in the town hall on Thursday evenings. For a moment, he considered going along, but then he put the idea out of his head as he turned and walked away.

"Dance classes?" he muttered under his breath. "Fat chance."

***

"I saw your lady friend the other day," Willy Bailey said a short while later, leaning back in his seat in the corner of the pub and taking a drag from his cigarette. "That nurse. What was her name again? Oh, that's right, Hazel Christie."

"She's not my lady friend," Johnny replied, unable to hide a sense of irritation. "She's just someone I know, that's all."

"Someone you took to the pictures a couple of times."

"That was a long time ago," Johnny pointed out, "and in case you didn't notice, she's married now. She's got a kid."

"She married that weirdo, right?" Willy asked. He took another puff. "The one who washed up on the night of the *Mercy Belle* disaster. I mean, who in their right mind marries a guy who just showed up like that? Hell, who marries a man who doesn't even know his own name? Is it even legal to do that?"

"It's one thing to nurse someone back to health," their friend Harry said. "It's quite another to actually marry the fellow."

"I can't believe he's still here," Willy

continued. "I mean, I get that he doesn't remember who he is, so he has nowhere else to go, but it's kind of ghoulish to have him living right here in Crowford. Every time I see him around, I find myself getting the willies. Which I guess is kind of appropriate, given my name."

"It's gotta hurt, though," Harry said, leaning across the table with a big grin, watching Johnny's reaction. "You always had the hots for Hazel, right from when we were kids. And then, just when you were getting ready to make your move, this stranger from out of town literally floats in and whisks her off her feet. Boom! Before you know it, she's marrying the guy and having his baby. Come on, Johnny, I'm not trying to rub it in here, but that has to really keep you awake at night. Especially since he's not exactly what you'd call a looker."

"Hey, knock it off," Willy said, nudging Harry in the arm. "Are you trying to drive the poor chap down even further than he already is?"

"I'm fine," Johnny replied, before taking a long drink from his pint glass. "I'm happy for her. She's happy, and that's all that matters. If you can't be happy for someone when they're happy, then what kind of person does that make you? She's happy with that Edward guy and that's all that matters."

"You said the word happy an awful lot just now," Harry continued, "for a guy who looks like he wants to put a rope round his neck and jump off the end of the pier."

Johnny turned and glared at him.

"Do you think he'll show up at the ceremony this evening?" Willy asked. "I can see why he might want to stay away. After all, tonight marks the fifth anniversary of the *Mercy Belle* disaster, so it's five years since Edward turned up here. If I was him, I wouldn't want to show my face, not since so many people are still sore over the fact that he survived and three local men didn't. I'm not saying it's his fault, but still..."

"It might look bad if he doesn't show, though," Harry pointed out. "People might think he doesn't care."

"I don't like seeing him," Willy muttered. "His face is disgusting. All those scars make him look like..."

His voice trailed off for a moment.

"Well, it's just not right," he continued finally. "He shouldn't be out in public. He should be, I don't know, living in a bell tower in Paris, or beneath an opera house."

"Listen to the pair of you," Johnny said with a sigh, "you're gossiping like a couple of old women. Who cares if Edward shows up or not? Today's about Crowford, and about what we lost. Edward's still an outsider, even after five years. If he wants to be accepted here, he should at least make some more effort to figure out his real name, instead of just using a name that he plucked out of thin air. That's why no-one really likes him. He has this air of deception, like he's not really who he says he is. It's no surprise that people are uncomfortable with that."

"Hazel Christie obviously doesn't mind so much," Harry said with a grin. "After all, she married the chap."

"Knock it off!" Willy hissed.

"No, it's fine," Johnny said, downing the rest of his pint before wiping his lips and getting to his feet. "I've got to go, anyway."

"Ignore Harry," Willy continued. "Everyone else does. He's just trying to wind you up, that's all."

"I have a lot to do today," Johnny explained as he stepped around the table, "but I'll see you guys this evening at the memorial." He paused for a moment. "I can't believe it's already been five years since that night. Time really flies past, doesn't it?"

"Chin up, man," Willy said. "I mean that. Don't let it get to you."

Once he was out of the pub, Johnny stopped for a moment and took a deep breath. He'd lied when he said he had a lot to do, and now he found himself at a bit of a loss. He looked around, wondering what he could do to fill the hours until the evening ceremony. He knew that getting drunk wasn't really a good idea, not when the evening was going to be so solemn, but there was precious little else for him to do in a small town like Crowford. He didn't fancy spending any more time with Willy and Harry, though, so he set off to find a different pub.

One where, hopefully, he'd be left alone for a few hours.

CHAPTER FIVE

"FATHER WARDEN?"

Startled, Father Warden looked up from his desk and saw Edith standing in the doorway.

"I'm so sorry," she continued, "I didn't mean to make you jump."

"No, it's fine," he murmured, even though he was feeling profoundly disturbed and unsettled. "I was just in a world of my own, I was trying to..."

His voice trailed off as he looked down at his notes. He'd been working on some words for the ceremony, but so far he'd been unable to really come up with anything meaningful or profound to say about the *Mercy Belle* disaster. In fact, all he'd managed to write after a couple of hours' work were a few bland opening remarks. He felt immense pressure to come up with something truly moving, something that would sum up the terrible impact of the disaster on the town, and so far he'd failed miserably.

"I was trying to finish my speech," he said finally, a little helplessly, as he looked over at Edith again. "For this evening."

"Of course," she said, with a hint of tears in her eyes. "I'm sure you'll more than do it justice. I've spoken to two people just this morning who mentioned how much they're looking forward to hearing you speak tonight. I'm sure you'll find a way to put everything into perspective, and to heal the pain that so many in our little town still feel. I must admit, I haven't been able to stop thinking about it all morning."

"Hmm," Father Warden replied, as he felt ten thousand extra tons of pressure landing on his already buckling shoulders.

"I'll leave you to it," she said. "I just wanted to know whether you'd like another cup of tea, that's all."

"I would indeed," he said, grateful for at least one moment of normality, "thank you."

He waited until she'd walked away, and then he looked back down at the sheet of paper. He'd actually managed to get a couple of lines done earlier, but then he'd come to the part where he'd specifically mentioned the five year anniversary, and that had been the moment at which his thoughts had come to a grinding halt. He still remembered every agonizing moment of that night when the *Mercy Belle* had been destroyed by a storm, but his thoughts quickly turned to the unsettling incident that had occurred later, when he'd encountered what had appeared to be the ghost of Captain John Lund.

For a few days, he'd told everyone who would listen about Lund's grave warning, but eventually he'd realized that he was being treated like a madman. He'd reached a point at which he'd felt that he was in danger of being removed from his position at the church, and that was when he'd decided to keep his mouth shut. Ever since, he'd been pondering the possibilities and praying for guidance and quietly dreading the fifth anniversary of the disaster. He kept telling himself that there was no real reason to worry, that the anniversary would come and go with no trouble, that ghosts didn't really exist.

And yet...

"Get a grip, man," he muttered to himself, hoping to strengthen his resolve. "You're supposed to provide comfort for the people of Crowford, not..."

Suddenly feeling something in his mouth, he reached up and wiped his lips. Looking down, he was surprised to see that several small particles were now smeared against the side of his hand. The particles looked, somehow, to be grains of sand.

"Errant nonsense," he said with a sigh, ignoring the rumbling sense of fear in his belly as he picked up his pen and tried to get back to work. "I shall not fall prey to idiotic superstitions."

He brushed the sand aside and got back to work, but a moment later he felt more particles around the tip of his tongue. These, too, he wiped away, but now he was becoming aware of a sense of great discomfort at the back of his throat. He coughed, then he coughed again, and finally he had no choice but to spit out another, slightly larger collection of sand. Some of the grains sprinkled down onto the paper as Father Warden sat back and tried to bring up the last of the grains.

Getting to his feet, he made his way out of the office and through to the little kitchen, where he poured himself a glass of water and then swilled his mouth. He spat the water out, and then he rinsed twice more, and each time he saw a small but disturbing quantity of sand mixed in with the water.

"This is impossible," he told himself out loud, and after a few seconds he realized that the sensation of sand in his mouth was beginning to fade.

He waited, still worried that more might come, and then he turned and began to make his way back through to the office. A little unsteady on his feet now, and most certainly startled, he continually ran his tongue around his mouth, searching for any sign that the sand had returned. By the time he was settled behind his desk, however, there had been no return of the sand, and he took a series of steady breaths as he looked down at his notes and realized that he was in danger of neglecting the task at hand.

"I'm sure you'll find a way to put everything into perspective," he remembered Edith saying, just a few minutes earlier, "and to heal the pain that so many in our little town still feel."

Those words now felt like a challenge, almost like a dare.

Reaching out, he picked up his pen and tried to work out what he should write next. It was at that moment, however, that he realized he could feel something uncomfortable in the back of his throat. He told himself that it could not possibly be more sand, and indeed after a few seconds he realized that this new 'thing' was in fact large and cold, and slippery too. Whatever it was, it seemed to be growing, until Father Warden set the pen back down and leaned forward, coughing and gagging in an attempt to clear his throat.

He gripped the edge of the desk with one hand, and with the fingers of the other he began to reach into his mouth in an attempt to clear the back of his throat from this strange new obstruction.

Letting out a series of pained gurgles, he struggled for a moment to find the object, but finally one fingertip wrapped around some kind of metal loop. Still utterly confused, Father Warden tried to pull the item out, only to feel a sharp pain at the very back of his tongue. Leaning forward, he let out a pained groan, but he knew that he had no choice but to proceed with the extraction. Even as saliva began to dribble from his lips, he forced himself to pull again on the loop, which now seemed to be slicing its way through his tongue. Finally, just as he was twisting the loop in an attempt to pull it free, he realized what he had discovered.

A fishing hook.

Somehow, impossibly, an actual fishing hook had somehow taken root at the back of his throat, and its barbed tip was firmly buried deep in the meat of his tongue. He tried to twist the hook this way and that in a desperate attempt to get it loose, but eventually he realized that he was going to have to pull hard. He took a moment to summon the strength that would be necessary, and then he forced himself to drag the hook out, cutting along the surface of his tongue until the barb sliced out and the hook fell down onto the desk, splattering the page with blood.

Tasting blood in his mouth, Father Warden stared down in horror at the sight of the hook, before – in a moment of panic – sliding the wretched thing into the waste paper basket.

He sat in silence, trying to work out where the hook had come from, but the whole situation made absolutely no sense whatsoever.

"Lord," he whispered, "grant me the strength to ignore this..."

Pausing, he tried to think of the right words.

"This provocation," he added finally. "Grant me the strength to work."

He quickly scrunched the piece of paper up and threw it in after the hook, and then he grabbed his pen and once again set about writing his speech. He had no idea how a fishing hook, of all things, could have ended up stuck in his tongue, but he was in no mood to try to fathom the unfathomable. He was half terrified that he might be losing his mind, but he supposed that was at least preferable to the idea that an actual fishing hook had somehow manifested in his mouth, or that he had produced sand along with saliva. Really, he thought, the best approach was to just get on with things.

After clearing his throat, he wrote out a couple more lines of his planned address, and then he paused again as he tried to come up with the next section.

Suddenly he let out a spluttering cough as he felt a sharp scratching sensation high up in the back of his nose, as if something was digging at the top of his nostrils He dropped the pen, which rolled off the desk and fell to the floor, and then he began to cough again as the scratching began to move slightly to the nostril on the right. He felt as if his entire nose was on the verge of swelling and splitting open, and the pain was excruciating as he felt tears being forced from his eyes and running down his face. He gasped, but the scratching was now moving down his right nostril, before finally a small, partly translucent crab-like creature fell down and landed with a plop on the piece of paper.

CHAPTER SIX

"EDWARD, DEAR, ARE YOU home?" Hazel called out as she maneuvered the pram into the hallway and then bumped the front door shut. "Tobias slept almost the whole way, can you believe that? He's such a good boy!"

Once she'd removed her coat, she began to lift the baby out of the pram. Tobias stirred slightly, but he was still – mostly – asleep as Hazel carried him through to the kitchen, where Edward was sitting at the table.

"Dear?" Hazel continued, surprised to find her husband sitting so still and quiet. "Are you alright? I thought you were going to use your day off to do some work in the garden. Is that no longer the plan?"

She waited, but now she was starting to

realize that something really seemed to be wrong.

"Edward..."

"I'm fine," he replied, although his voice sounded very thin and weak. He turned to her with fear in his eyes. The rest of his face, though healed, was still terribly scarred, and there were bald patches all over his scalp where his hair had never grown back. "I was just collecting my thoughts."

"Perhaps today wasn't the right time to tackle a big job," she said, forcing a smile as she carried Tobias over to him. "Why don't you play for a while? It would do you both some good."

Edward stared at his own son with a curious expression, as if he felt slightly sickened.

"Edward," Hazel added after a moment, "today of all days -"

"I'm going to the ceremony tonight," he said, interrupting her.

She sighed.

"I'm going!" he said firmly.

"Edward, are you sure that's wise?"

"There's no good choice here," he continued. "You know that. If I go, everyone will stare at me and blame me. If I don't go, they'll think I'm cruel and uncaring. There's literally not one single choice that will make things better, so I have to do the only thing that I know is right." He paused. "Three men died that night. I should be there to remember it. So I'm going. At least that way, I'll be able to live with myself."

"Edward..."

She took a seat opposite him, while still gently cradling Tobias in her arms. She seemed uncertain as to what she might say next, although she desperately wanted to make her husband feel better. That was all she'd ever wanted, since she'd first met him.

"Do you know how many people came into the repair shop today?" Edward asked. "Zero. No-one came in, and it's been like that all way. Arnold didn't say anything, and I'm still so grateful to him for taking a risk and giving me a job, but we both know what's happening. Me being there is depressing his trade, and I can't let that happen, not to a man as good as Arnold. His business shouldn't suffer on account of me."

"I'm sure you're overreacting."

"I'm not. I know that even before the anniversary rolled around, some people were already avoiding the place on account of..."

He paused, and then he reached up and touched the knotted scars that made up what was left of his face. Lacking a nose and ears, he had at least retained his sight, although sometimes he wished that he'd never been able to see the full extent of his injuries. Sometimes he caught himself wondering whether he was glad he'd survived at all. He felt bad for such thoughts, of course, since he was so utterly grateful to have Hazel and now Tobias in his life. Still, there were moments when he wondered about the cost of his happiness.

"I'm not welcome here," he continued finally. "I remind people of what happened. Tonight more than ever, they're going to all be talking about me."

"It'll get better next week, once..."

Her voice trailed off.

"Once the anniversary is out of the way?" He stared at her for a moment, before shaking his head and getting to his feet. "This town is never going to forget the tragedy of the *Mercy Belle*, and they *shouldn't* forget it. Them remembering what happened is not the problem here, the problem is me! The problem is that I remind them of it, and some of them think I'm responsible, and I can't tell them I'm not responsible because I still don't remember what happened! I don't remember being on that boat on that awful night and -"

"Edward, please..."

"And I don't remember who I am!" he snapped, banging a fist against the table.

Immediately, Tobias began to cry.

"It's okay, darling," Hazel said as she tried to rock him back to sleep. "Daddy's not cross. He's just a little upset about something."

"I'm going out," Edward muttered, stepping past them and heading to the door.

"Where?"
"Just out!"

***

Stopping as he finally reached his patch on the allotment, Edward took a deep breath and tried to calm his racing mind. He usually found peace on the allotment, but today something felt different. He looked around at the backs of all the houses that surrounded the space, high above at the tops of the slopes that bordered the sunken space, and he felt certain that he was being watched.

"I'm going out," he heard his own voice snapping, echoing in his thoughts from just a short time earlier.

"Where?" Hazel had asked.

"Just out!"

"But -"

"I told you, I'm going out!"

With that, he'd slammed the door. Now he felt awful, and he hated himself for being so sharp with his wife. Hazel was the most caring woman he'd ever met, and he knew that she'd sacrificed a lot when she'd agreed to marry him. He felt supremely lucky to have her in his life; other times, however, this sense of luck was tempered by the fear that he was dragging her down, as if she'd be better off without him. After all, she'd once been so popular in the town, whereas now she was viewed with suspicion because of her marriage.

Because of me, he caught himself thinking.

Looking down at the plot, he tried to busy himself with thoughts of all the work that would need doing in the spring. He'd prepped the ground well for the winter, and now there was little to do other than wait. Waiting, however, was an interminable grind that allowed his mind to fill with dangerous thoughts, and he was already starting to think about the memorial ceremony that was going to take place in the evening. He'd decided, after weeks of prevarication, that' he'd definitely attend, although now he was once again starting to have doubts.

There were still moments when he tried to remember.

Spotting some broken glass in the mud, he reached down and picked it up. One of the jars had managed to get smashed, most likely knocked over by the rain.

Even now, standing alone in the allotment, Edward imagined himself standing on the deck of the *Mercy Belle*, with the storm raging all around. He'd seen enough photographs to know roughly what the boat must have looked like on that awful night, and he'd seen pictures of the crew as well. He imagined Captain Lund shouting at him, although he couldn't imagine what the man was shouting *about*. He hoped that, by thinking of what that night must have been like, he might eventually trick his brain into revealing the truth. Still, however, nothing came.

Five years.

Five long years had passed, and he'd never experienced so much as a sliver of memory regarding that awful night on the *Mercy Belle*. Now, for the first time, he felt as if he remembered the sensation of being on the boat's swaying deck, and there had been something else too: for a moment, he felt the memory of rain falling against his face, of the storm that had destroyed the *Mercy Belle*. All he wanted was one tiny thread, one hint of the truth, so that he could begin to unravel everything that had happened, but after a moment he realized that these memories weren't memories at all. He was fooling himself.

His memory wasn't going to suddenly, miraculously unlock.

He'd come to terms with the fact that he was never going to remember what had happened on the boat that night, or anything about his life prior to that moment when he'd woken up in Doctor Ford's surgery and seen Hazel's beautiful face staring back at him. He was condemned to the amnesia, and he was starting to realize that he would never remember the truth about who he was, or about how he had ended up on the *Mercy Belle* on that fateful night. That didn't make it easy, though, and it didn't mean that he wasn't horrified by the thought of being hated by the whole town. So many times, he'd resolved to leave Crowford and start afresh somewhere else, but Hazel had been so kind and loving to him, and he knew he could never leave her. Besides, he truly, genuinely loved her, and Tobias too.

But how could he live in a place where everyone thought he was responsible for such a terrible tragedy?

Suddenly, feeling a sharp pain in his right hand, he looked down and saw that he'd inadvertently formed a fist and begun to squeeze tight. The shard of broken glass, from the jar, had sliced deep into his palm, and he hadn't even noticed. Now blood was dribbling down to his wrist and then falling down onto the muddy ground.

CHAPTER SEVEN

BY THE TIME 6PM rolled around, and darkness had fallen across Crowford, a crowd had begun to gather outside the town hall. The Crowford Shanty Choir had started to perform, regaling the crowd with local songs of the sea. People were talking nervously, many of them sharing memories of the night five years earlier when the *Mercy Belle* had gone down. Almost everyone in town had either known the three dead men, or had in some way been connected – at least tangentially – to the fishing fleet that had for many years been the pride of Crowford.

The tragedy had only reinforced that bond, and the sense that Crowford was defined by its position perched on the coast.

"This must be pretty strange for you," Willy

said as he, Harry and Johnny joined the back of the crowd, from where they could easily see the stage where the speakers were due to stand. He turned to Johnny. "I mean, what with you having been one of the ones who went out there and found what had happened."

"It's a shame old Manners isn't coming," Johnny replied. "He'd have had plenty to say, I'm sure."

"He's almost drunk himself to death, hasn't he?" Willy asked. "That's what I heard, anyway. That he never really recovered from seeing the debris of the *Mercy Belle* out there on the waves. I know he resigned his post on the lifeboat pretty soon after."

Before Johnny could reply, he spotted a familiar figure over at the other end of the crowd. Hazel had arrived, pushing Tobias in his pram. For a moment, Johnny felt that he should go over and speak to her, but then he saw that she wasn't alone. Edward was with her, although he seemed to be holding back a little, keeping to the shadows of the Red Cow public house as if he didn't want to be seen.

If that was Edward's intention, however, it didn't seem to be working.

Slowly, more and more people began to notice his arrival. Nobody wanted to stare, of course, but many people pretended to be turning and glancing at something else so that they could catch a glimpse of the man whose arrival five years earlier had been part of the *Mercy Belle* story. For his part, Edward had already decided that he would ignore all the gawping, and even now he was resolutely looking toward the stage and waiting for the first speech, and trying to force himself to listen to the shanties.

"The *Mercy Belle* went down, she did," the choir sang, "deep down into the sands."

"He showed his face, then," Willy muttered darkly. "Well, what face he's got left, at least."

"It's not right, is it?" Harry added. "He turns up here and he immediately scoops up the prettiest girl in the whole town. She's only with him because she feels sorry for him."

Suddenly Hazel happened to glance at them, and she and Johnny immediately made eye contact. An awkward pause ensued, which was finally broken when they both heard the sound of footsteps on the wooden stage. Johnny turned away first, just in time to see that Father Warden and a few other dignitaries were taking their places. Although they had once been volunteers together on the *James Furnham*, Johnny and Father Warden had not seen one another very much over the years, and he was immediately struck by the older man's haunted, jittery expression. It was as if Father Warden had aged many years more than he should.

"I just realized," Harry said, "this is going to be really boring, isn't it? We're going to the pub after, right? I don't care which pub, I just need a few pints."

The choir came to the end of their latest shanty, and then they took their seats.

All across the crowd, a strange silence began to fall. A few people still whispered to one another, but on the stage Father Warden was discussing some last-minute technicalities with Mayor Kidd. Behind them, the town's most recent war memorial stood bathed in darkness, bearing the names of all those from the town who had been killed in the Second World War just ten years previously. The open square at the front of the town hall had long been the heart of Crowford, so naturally it was also the spot where the people of the town gathered to remember past tragedies. The sinking of the *Mercy Belle* had already been ordained as one of Crowford's most awful stories.

Up on the stage, looking out across the crowd, Father Warden realized that the time had come.

He at least had managed to finish his speech, even if he felt that he might have done better in other circumstances. In truth, all afternoon he had continued to be troubled by strange occurrences that had kept him distracted. After the little crab-like creature had fallen from his nose, he'd been unable to shake the sensation of something scratching at the back of his throat, although mercifully no more actual crabs had emerged. Still, he couldn't help but worry that perhaps the crab had laid some eggs – or whatever crabs did – and that he should speak to Doctor Ford at some point. He'd also experienced several coughing fits, during which he'd found himself bringing up more small quantities of sand.

And then there had been the smudges.

Several times, throughout the afternoon, he'd noticed faint smudge-like shapes at the edge of his vision. These smudges were tall, perhaps human-sized, but they immediately vanished whenever Father Warden actually tried to look directly at them. He'd been trying to convince himself that they weren't real at all, but if anything they'd become more persistent as night had fallen.

Now, as he approached the lectern, Father Warden knew that – for the sake of the town – he had to find some way to calm his nerves and deliver some kind of comfort.

As he looked out across the crowd, he saw a couple of hundred faces staring back at him. Never in all his time in Crowford had he felt so needed, so necessary to the town's spiritual well-being, and from somewhere deep inside he felt a kind of strength growing. He was going to make these people feel better, and he was going to ensure that the tragedy of the *Mercy Belle* could be used to strengthen the town, rather than letting it drag everybody down. This was going to be a turning point. He set his notes on the lectern, he took a deep breath, and finally he looked once more at all the faces and he opened his mouth to start.

And then he froze.

Captain John Lund, former captain of the *Mercy Belle* and a man who had been dead for five years, was staring back at him from the rear of the crowd.

Seemingly unnoticed by anybody else, Lund and the two other dead men from that night – Keith Simmons and Percy Weaver – stood in the shadows. Their eyes were fixed on Father Warden, and they were watching him with expressions of what seemed to be a kind of solemn disgust. Disappointment, perhaps.

"Ladies and gentlemen," Father Warden stammered, determined to begin his speech, and hoping that by doing so he might banish the three ghosts, "we are gathered here today because we are united by a sense of profound loss. Five years ago on this very night, our town suffered a tragedy that claimed three of our sons. Captain John -"

Stopping suddenly, he found himself looking directly at the very man he had been about to eulogize. Captain John Lund – or, at least, the ghost of Captain John Lund – stood with gray features and waited for Father Warden to continue. Although he felt that he could not go on, Father Warden also knew that he must be hallucinating the three figures, since nobody else in the crowd was able to see them. He certainly couldn't raise the alarm, not without reigniting concerns about his mental state. He resolved, therefore, to simply ignore the three dead men, and to hope that they would soon go away.

"Are you alright?"

Turning, Father Warden saw that Mayor Kidd was leaning forward slightly in his chair. Seated next to him was Eric Grace, a local businessman, who had brought his daughters Angela and Vivian along. Several other Crowford bigwigs had also wheedled their way onto the stage.

"I'm fine," Father Warden stammered, keen to not make a fuss. He began to force a smile, only to abandon it at the last moment as he realized how unconvincing it would seem. "Just a little overcome, that's all."

He turned back to look at the crowd, and he immediately saw that the three dead men were gone. He glanced around, convinced that he would soon see them again, and then he felt a rush of relief as he realized that they genuinely seemed to have left. He took a deep breath, regained his composure, and finally told himself that he was ready to make the speech that the town wanted to hear.

"Ladies and gentlemen, I shall start again," he announced, before clearing his throat. "We are gathered here today because we are united by a sense of profound loss. Five years ago on this very night, our town suffered a tragedy that claimed the lives of three of our sons."

CHAPTER EIGHT

"THAT WAS BEAUTIFUL," Hazel said as she pushed the pram away from the stage, once the speeches were over. The shanties had resumed, ringing out across the town. "It was very moving. Don't you think so?"

She glanced at Edward, waiting for him to say something, but she immediately saw that he was lost in his own thoughts. She'd been worried about him all day, and now she was starting to realize that perhaps he should have stayed away from the ceremony after all. He'd hardly been paying attention, anyway; she'd noticed that faraway look in his eyes during all the speeches.

"So I was thinking," she continued, hoping to jog him into the conversation, "we should get out of town for a few hours. Do you want to take a trip into the countryside at the weekend? We could go for a nice walk, let Tobias experience some nature, that sort of thing. He's never really seen much beyond the confines of the town, has he? I mean, there *is* more to life than just the streets of Crowford."

Again she waited, and again her husband showed no sign that he'd even heard a word that she'd just said.

"It might be good for *us*, too," she added. "We could just get away from things and -"

"I'm going for a walk," he said suddenly, stopping at the street corner.

"Now?" she asked incredulously.

"I need to clear my head. I need to go for a walk."

"But we *are* walking. Together. As a family."

"You know what I mean."

"I think maybe we need to talk," she told him. "Darling, it's okay to feel uneasy, today of all days. This was always going to be a difficult milestone for you to mark."

"Did you see how everyone was looking at me?"

"I'm really not sure that they were actually -"

"Don't lie to me!" he snapped suddenly, before taking a deep breath. "I'm sorry, I didn't mean that to sound the way it did."

"Okay, so a few busybodies were looking at you," she replied. "Does that matter? It says a lot more about them, than it does about you, or about us. Crowford is a pretty small place, and small places breed gossip. So what if a few nosy people have nothing better to do with their time than worry about what everyone else is doing? They don't matter to us, not really."

"When I first woke up here," he said, "I never thought that I'd stay. Then it turned out that I had nowhere to go, and then you and I grew closer, but sometimes I think that for the good of the people here, I should have cleared off. The longer I'm here, the longer they're faced – every day – with a reminder of the fact that the *Mercy Belle* was lost. It's like they're all expecting me to remember what happened, so I can tell them and clear up the big mystery. But I'm not going to remember, am I? Not after all this time."

"You shouldn't put so much pressure on yourself. It won't help."

He took a step back, as the sea shanties continued in the distance.

"Let's go home," Hazel continued, "and -"

"I just need to get my head together."

"I'm your wife and helping you with that is my job," she said, stepping over to him and putting a hand on the side of his arm. "We'll go home and have a nice cup of tea, and you can tell me everything that's on your mind." She paused, watching his face for any hint of a clue as to how he was really feeling. "Edward," she added cautiously, "you're not... I don't mean to pressure you, but you're not starting to remember anything, are you?"

"No!" he snapped quickly. "Why would you think that?"

"I don't, not really," she replied, before spotting a familiar figure walking past. "I suppose I just want to know what's going on in that head of yours. Darling, I just want to go and talk to Daphne about something, and then I'll be right back. Do you mind waiting here with Tobias?"

"Sure," he muttered. "Whatever."

"I'll only be a couple of minutes," she added. "Then we can go home together. As a family."

As Hazel hurried over to speak to her friend, Edward looked down into the pram and saw Tobias staring back up at him. Unable to stifle a faint smile at the sight of his son, he reached into the pram and touched the boy's noise, causing Tobias to let out an excited gurgle. No matter how proud he felt, however, Edward still couldn't quite shake the feeling that he was somehow inadequate as a father, or that Tobias would suffer in Crowford as a result. There were times when he genuinely felt that the best thing he could do – as a father *and* as a husband – would be to simply disappear.

"What the hell are you doing here?" a voice screamed suddenly.

Startled, Edward looked around, but he already knew that the voice hadn't been real. Or, rather, it had been real once, but now it was simply some kind of echo that had briefly invaded his mind. The voice had seemed familiar, even if he couldn't quite place it, and it had been accompanied by the incongruous sound of crashing rain and waves. For a moment, he'd even felt as if his feet were a little unsteady, almost as if he'd been standing on the deck of a boat, except he'd made a point of not going on boats so he didn't even know how he could remember that sensation.

Unless...

A sense of dread began to creep through his chest, like a slowly rising tide. A moment earlier, Hazel had asked him if he was remembering anything about his past, and he'd told the truth when he'd insisted that nothing was coming back to him. Now, however, he began to realize that the strange voice had most definitely felt like a memory, even if it was one that had arrived with absolutely no context. Was it possible, he wondered, that after five years he was finally starting to remember what had happened on that fateful night aboard the *Mercy Belle*? Although he'd long *hoped* to remember, now the thought was absolutely terrifying.

"Hello there, Edward," Mrs. Carter said as she stopped and looked down at Tobias. "Might I say hello to the little fellow?"

"Of course," he murmured, stepping back so that she could get a better look, although his mind was racing and he was terrified that another memory might arrive at any moment. He wanted so badly to remember, but now he wasn't sure that the time was quite right.

"He's so lovely," Mrs. Carter continued. "Aren't you, Tobias? Yes, you're an absolutely delight! I'm sure your parents are so proud of you!"

"We are," Edward said, but he was barely paying attention to the woman, and after a moment he took another step back. "Tell Hazel I'll see her at home."

"I beg your pardon?" Mrs. Carter asked, turning to him.

"I'll see her at home," he continued, struggling to hide the sense of panic from his voice. "Just tell her that, okay? Tell her I'm fine, but that I need to clear my head. Tell her not to worry."

"Well, I -"

Before Mrs. Carter could say another word, Edward turned and hurried away, quickly slipping into the crowd so that he wouldn't be spotted by his wife. He knew that she'd fret over him, but he couldn't contemplate the idea of going home, not when he was worried that he might be on the verge of remembering his past. For that, he needed to be completely alone, not only for his sake but also for Hazel and Tobias too. He was worried about how he might react to anything he remembered, and the last thing he wanted was for his wife and son to get hurt.

"What the hell are you doing here?"

That voice was echoing through his thoughts now, again and again, and it seemed to be trailing a memory that he just couldn't quite grasp. The tide in his mind was getting higher, but still not high enough.

"What the hell are you doing here?"

"What the hell are you doing here?"

"What the hell are you doing here?"

No matter how many times he ran those words through his mind, he felt as if he was still just slightly too far from any moment of realization. He was torn between wanting to know, on the one hand, and feeling abject terror on the other. He'd always wondered what would happen if his memory suddenly returned, and now he was worried that he might find that he wasn't the kind of man he thought he was. After all, he'd apparently turned up somehow out of the blue on the deck of the *Mercy Belle*, which made very little sense. How was that possible?

Reaching the edge of the crowd, he momentarily wondered exactly where he could go in order to be alone. A moment later he realized that there was only one option, so he hurried along Queen Street and quickly disappeared into the shadows.

CHAPTER NINE

"WELL, I WAS RIGHT," Harry said a couple of hours later in the Star and Garter pub, before taking a sip from his pint of beer, "that *was* boring. I honestly thought old Warden wasn't ever going to shut up. And I never want to hear another sea shanty, not for as long as I live."

"Warden didn't seem too perky," Willy pointed out. "Did you see his face, especially at the start? He looked like he was about to keel over."

"Did you get a chance to speak to him?" Harry asked, turning to Johnny.

"Me?" Johnny hesitated, having been a little zoned out for a moment. It took him a couple of seconds to realize what he'd been asked. "No. No, I didn't. Another time."

"Hey, look who's walking past! Willy said,

craning his neck to look out the window.

Turning, Johnny saw a familiar figure wandering along the dark street. There was something about the limp, about the hunched shoulders, about the slightly cowed gait that immediately marked out Edward Smith. The man opened a gate and made his way down the steps into the allotment, and a moment later he'd disappeared from sight.

"What's he doing down there at this time of night?" Willy asked.

"He's weird one, that's for sure," Harry added. "I don't trust anyone who goes slinking about late in the dark like that."

"I'm sure he's got his reasons," Johnny suggested.

"Yeah?" Willy hesitated, before downing the last of his beer. "It's almost kicking out time anyway, we won't get served another. Why don't we go and see exactly what that freak's up to?"

Johnny sighed.

"We're supposed to be up early tomorrow, remember?" he reminded them. "We're going out to the sands with my uncle."

"It still wouldn't hurt to keep an eye on him," Harry said, as he too finished his beer. He nudged Johnny. "You coming?"

"Who cares what he's doing out there?" Johnny asked, sounding tired. "Haven't we all got better things to do?"

Harry and Willy were already bundling out the door, and Johnny let out another sigh as he realized that they hadn't even heard him. He had no interest whatsoever in going down to the allotment, but he supposed that someone should at least keep an eye on things. After all, Harry and Willy were pretty drunk, and they'd both had antsy moments in the past. Finally, although he felt exhausted, Johnny hauled himself up and headed off to follow his friends.

***

"Hey, mate! Mate, slow down, we only wanna talk to you! Oi! Slow down there!"

As he reached his plot on the allotment, Edward turned to see two figures making their way down the dirt path that led from the street, and a moment later he saw that a third figure was following a little way back. Instantly tensing, Edward looked around to make sure that there was nobody else nearby, and then he told himself to stay calm. He could handle a few local drunks. He'd always managed to handle their kind in the past.

All he wanted was to be alone, so that he could wait to see if his memories began to return.

"Mate, relax," Willy said as he got closer. "We're not here to cause any trouble. We just saw you out here and we wondered if we might be of assistance."

"Yeah, that's all we wondered," Harry said, a little breathless from the pursuit. "You don't often see a fellow out and about this late, all by himself. In a town like Crowford, everyone has a responsibility to keep an eye out and make sure that nobody's getting up to any mischief. We thought we'd come and see whether anything's wrong, that's all."

"Nothing's wrong," Edward replied, his scarred face picked out by the moonlight. "I just came down to check on a few things."

"This late?" Harry asked.

"This late."

Edward hesitated, and then he spotted Johnny making his way over. Something about Johnny always set Edward on edge, not only because Johnny had been one of the first faces he'd seen after losing his memory, but also because he'd long sensed a kind of frisson of excitement between Johnny and Hazel. He knew they'd been close, once. Even now, just seeing Johnny's face caused Edward to involuntarily start clenching his fists, although he quickly stopped himself.

Not quickly enough, however.

The other three men had all noticed.

"Like I said, calm down," Harry continued. "We don't want to make war with you, my friend, we just -"

"I'm not your friend," Edward replied, interrupting him.

"Well, that's kinda hostile," Harry said.

"I came down here to be alone," Edward explained. "I'm not harming anyone, I just want to be left alone with my thoughts for a while."

He waited, but for a few seconds nobody responded.

"You know," Harry said finally, "it's really not your face that makes us not like you. We've all seen faces like yours before. Hell, ten years ago when the war ended, we all saw men come back with horrible injuries, even worse than what you've got going on." He paused, and then he took a step forward. "I suppose that's part of the problem here, really. You've got the kind of injuries that a man gets from war, from doing the right thing and fighting for his country, but that's not what happened to you, is it? No, you just caused one of our town's boats to sink, you caused the deaths of three men and -"

"I didn't cause any of that!" Edward snapped angrily.

"Calm down," Harry said, holding his hands up. "No need to get aggressive. I'm just pointing out that you look like something you're not. A soldier. A hero. And what you really are, if you'll pardon my language for a moment, is a miserable son of a bitch who came to our town, took advantage of our hospitality, and even married one of our girls."

"Leave Hazel out of this!" Edward sneered, stepping toward him until they were almost chest-to-chest.

"I'm just pointing out the facts," Harry continued. "No-one likes a chap who takes things that shouldn't rightfully belong to them."

"Let's go," Johnny said. "We shouldn't even be here."

"I never asked anyone for anything!" Edward said firmly. "The people of Crowford have been so good to me, they healed me and I was given a job and -"

"And you took a woman for yourself."

"I didn't take anyone! We fell in love!"

"Is it love," Harry replied with a smile, "or is it pity?"

"Take that back!" Unable to control himself for a moment longer, Edward lunged at Harry, shoving him with such force that he sent him falling to the ground.

"Easy there!" Willy said, pushing Edward in the chest. "That's no way to react to a simple conversation!"

"Leave me alone!" Edward yelled.

"This is public property," Willy pointed out, as Harry stood back up. "It's owned by the town, which means anyone's allowed to come down here.

You're not from round here, so you sure as hell don't get to tell us what to do in our own -"

Before he could finish, they all heard the tell-tale sound of a flick-knife being opened, and a second later Harry stepped forward with the blade held up for everyone to see.

"You want to get into a spot of trouble tonight?" he asked Edward. "Okay, here's some trouble!"

Lunging forward, he slashed the knife toward Edward's face, only to let out a gasp as he was pulled back at the last moment. Johnny had grabbed him by the shoulders, and a moment later he sent Harry scrambling back across the muddy ground.

"Cut it out!" Johnny shouted.

"I was only -"

"You were only *what*?" Johnny asked, interrupting him. "Were you going to stab him? Is that it?"

"No, I -"

"Then put the knife away!"

Harry hesitated, before doing as he was told.

"This night is over," Johnny continued, turning to each of the other men in turn. "No-one's going to start waving knives around, okay? There's only one way that kind of thing ends, and it's not good. Sure, we're not happy about things, but there's a limit. Harry, Willy, we're going home. You got that?"

"You're a lucky man," Harry said to Edward. "Another time, you might have ended up with some more scars to add to your collection."

"Bring it on," Edward sneered. "You're nothing but a coward, anyway."

"Move!" Johnny said, shoving Harry in the back, forcing him to head toward the path. "It's late, it's cold, and I'm sick of all this bullshit!"

Left alone, Edward watched as the three men left. Johnny glanced back at him, but Edward simply stared at him sternly, until finally the three of them were gone. Taking a deep breath, Edward stood all alone in the middle of the allotment and, as he waited for more memories to return, he listened to the sound of trees rustling in the distance. He could hear the sea, too, as the sound of the waves reverberated throughout the town. Looking all around in the darkness, Edward listened to the sound of waves crashing against the shore, but that sound seemed to be everywhere all at once, bouncing off the walls of all the houses. In Crowford, no-one was ever really able to escape the sea.

CHAPTER TEN

"GOODNIGHT, FATHER WARDEN," Edith said as she stepped into her hallway and turned back to him. "Thank you ever so much for walking me home. You're such a gentleman."

"It was my pleasure," he replied, with a faint smile and a nod of the head. "I couldn't let you be out in these dark streets alone, could I?"

"I don't think much bad could happen to me in Crowford. I've never felt safer anywhere."

"Still, best to be sure," he added, before taking a step back. "Goodnight, and I shall see you bright and early in the morning. Don't forget, we need to sort through those hymn books and ensure that they're ready for the service on Sunday."

With that, he turned and made his way along the dark street. He was feeling a little better now, having managed to deliver his speech, and he was just about managing to dredge up some optimism. Over the previous few weeks, he'd been extremely worried about the approaching fifth anniversary of the *Mercy Belle* disaster, but finally he was starting to cast aside his superstitions. As for the strange occurrences in his office, when he'd spit up sand and a little crab and whatnot, he was starting to write those off as small hallucinations.

Nothing to worry about, then.

Father Walter Warden was not, by habit, a very curious man, and he was more than capable of believing anything that made him feel a little better.

As he headed around the next corner, however, he was suddenly struck by the sensation that he was being watched. He stopped and looked over his shoulder, but there was no sign of anyone, and the only sound came from the roar of distant waves crashing against the beach. He hesitated, just to make sure that there was no reason to worry, and then he set off again. He was still a few minutes from home, but already he was reaching into his pocket for his keys, so that he'd be able to get inside quickly. The nagging sense of being watched had still not gone away.

By the time he reached his front door, he was staring to shake with fear. He didn't even know why; he was simply overwhelmed by a sense that something awful was about to happen. Indeed, his hands were trembling so badly, he struggled for a moment to even get the key into the lock.

"Come on," he muttered to himself under his breath. "Don't be a silly old fool."

Once the door was open, he hurried inside and pushed it shut again, and then he stood for a few seconds in the dark hallway as he tried to get his thoughts together. Almost immediately, however, he began to notice a strange smell in the air, a smell that was counter to the usual smell of his house. He sniffed, trying to work out what could be wrong, and he soon realized that what he could smell was a faintly salty, planktony aroma that was more common around the shoreline and, in particular, close to the legs of the pier whenever the tide happened to be out.

There was something else mixed in there, too. Something slightly rotten.

A moment later, hearing a faint squelching sound, he looked toward the open doorway that led into his front room. The smell of the sea was getting stronger and stronger, and he could still just about hear the sound of waves in the distance. He took a step forward, and then he stopped as he heard what seemed to be a buoy clanging somewhere far off out to sea, except... He was used to hearing the waves, but he knew that the sound of a buoy shouldn't carry so far. He felt an urge to run, but he reminded himself that this was his home, and after a few more seconds he forced himself to step over to the doorway and look into the front room.

Nothing.

There was nothing out of the ordinary in there at all. He saw only his furniture, all settled and ordered in the darkness, although the smell of the sea persisted. He told himself that there was no reason to be fearful, yet at the same time he still felt as if he was being watched.

Finally, he turned to go through to the kitchen, only to let out a gasp of shock as he saw that three figures were standing right behind him in the darkened hallway.

"He is ours," Captain John Lund said, his voice sounding scratchy and dry now. "We have waited. We will have him now."

"I... I..."

"You were warned," Captain Lund continued, taking a step forward. "He should not be here, not after what he did. If you will not deliver him to us, we will take him by force."

"No," Father Warden stammered, as he backed away against the wall, knocking a painting in the process, "please, you have to understand..."

"Five years," one of the other dead men said. "That's long enough for you to do what's right."

"But it's not up to me!" Father Warden told them, as he slithered down against the wall and bumped to the floor, from where he looked up at the three rotten figures. "If you want him, why don't you just go and take him?"

"He must be offered to us," Captain Lund replied, "so that we know this town respects the sea."

"If you won't be the one to do that," one of the others added, "then we will find someone who will."

"No!"

"And until we are satisfied," the third dead man said, "there will be no peace for Crowford, and no prosperity. All shall suffer until what's right is done."

"Starting with you," Captain Lund said darkly. "You had five years to deliver him, and you did not."

"I didn't know *I* had to do it!" Father Warden shouted, as the dead captain reached down and grabbed him by the throat. "Why me?"

"Because you were one of the ones who took him from us," Captain Lund replied. "Never fear, though. You were not the only one."

Before Father Warden could reply, he began to gasp for air. He felt cold, dirty water bubbling up at the back of his throat, and he realized that somehow – impossibly – he was starting to drown. No matter how hard he tried to spit the water out, more and more was rising up through his body with each passing second, even as Captain Lund let go of him and took a step back. His lungs had become some kind of great slimy pump, pushing seawater out through his entire body.

"Please!" Father Warden gurgled, but it was too late. Now he was swelling all over, as more dirty sea water filled him and began to split his skin open. "Not..."

Dropping onto his hands and knees, he tried to let all the water fall from his mouth, but there was simply too much. It wasn't only water, either; he could feel tiny creatures wriggling and twisting all through his body, as their legs scratched against the insides of his belly and lungs and throat. Some of the creatures quickly became larger, until he realized he was being chewed up from the inside. As more water bubbled in his mouth, he felt something sharp slicing through his guts and forcing its way up into his chest cavity. He was full, to the point of bursting, and when he looked down at his own hands he saw that they were swollen and misformed, as if they really might break open at any moment and leak water.

He tried one final time to cry out, before slumping down and falling dead against the floor. In that instant, the sheer pressure of water forced one of his eyeballs out of its socket, followed by scores of tiny mites.

Captain Lund and his men, meanwhile, were

now nowhere to be seen.

***

"What the -"

Startled awake, Reginald Manners – formerly *Captain* Reginald Manners of the *James Furnham* – quickly realized that he'd fallen asleep in his armchair.

Again.

The lights were off, and the whole living room stank of whiskey and beer. As soon as he began to move, Manners felt his feet bumping against beer bottles, and he slumped back in the chair with a heavy sigh. He let out another sigh as he tried to remember how he'd ended up drunk, and then he realized that it must have been the same old story. When, he wondered, was the last time he'd actually spent a whole day without taking a drink?

Four years, at least.

Almost five.

As a throbbing pain began to pound at the right side of his head, he made another effort to get to his feet, and this time he just about managed. He had to steady himself against the mantelpiece, and then he took a few seconds to wait for the dizziness to pass. That took a little longer than he expected, but he was used to waking up still drunk so he figured there was no real harm done. Besides, he had nothing else to be doing at...

He glanced at the clock on the mantelpiece.

1am.

He felt a rush of relief as he realized that technically the anniversary was over. The day had weighed heavy on him for a while, and he supposed he could use it as an excuse for his drunkenness. He'd need a new excuse the next day, though.

Sighing again, he turned and began to make his way to the kitchen, but he immediately bumped against the side of the dining table. A couple of glasses fell off the other end and smashed on the floor. Letting out a series of curses, Manners struggled to keep from falling down, but again he was able to stabilize himself and he quickly resumed his slow, wobbly shuffle across the room.

"He is ours," a voice said suddenly in the darkness. "You will deliver him to us."

Stopping, Manners told himself that he must be imagining things, but after a couple of seconds he realized that he could smell the sea. The stench was getting stronger by the second, and finally he turned and looked over his shoulder, only to see the ghostly face of Captain John Lund staring at him as the rotten, salty stench grew ever stronger.

"We will not relent," Captain Lund said gravely. "He is owed to the sea. Give him to us, or the town of Crowford will pay a terrible price."

CHAPTER ELEVEN

BRIGHT MORNING SUNLIGHT SPREAD across the sea, and across the bleached white sandbanks that were poking up above the water.

Five miles out from Crowford, the dunes were a rare spectacle that only appeared at low tide. They were the uppermost tip of a larger sandbank that stretched for a couple of miles in each direction. Over the years, the sands had claimed many vessels, with the result that the tops of a few old masts could be seen dotted around the area, marking the spots where ships – and in a lot of cases, their crews as well – had been entombed beneath the surface. It was not for nothing that the Crowford Sands had gained a formidable reputation over the centuries, and historians had estimated that more than ten thousand men had been lost to their deep clutches.

At the southern end of the largest exposed section, a fishing vessel named the Mary Sue lay anchored, and half a dozen men had climbed down to make their way across the sand. Each man was carrying a bucket, for the prize on that sunny day was a variety of tiny shrimp that lived only in the sandbanks, and which were prized all around the world for their exceptional quality. Restaurants from London to Paris, and from New York to Singapore, had been known to pay top price for a supply.

"You call this a good way to spend a morning?" Willy muttered, still heavily hungover from the night before. "I can think of better ways."

"There has to be more to life than shrimp," Harry added wearily. "I mean, why do people care about *these* particular ones so much, anyway? Are they made out of gold or something?"

"Apparently they're the best that money can buy," Johnny reminded them. He, too, was feeling worse for wear, although he was a little better at covering the fact. "If some rich buggers in London want to pay over the odds for this stuff, who are we to argue? Just remember not to step on the palest patches of sand, because that's the stuff that's dangerous." He turned to the others and smiled. "A man can be sucked under in ten seconds flat."

"It's too bright," Willy complained. "And it's

creepy, too."

"You mean the wrecks?"

Stopping, Johnny looked out at the nearest mast, which rose about ten feet above the surface of the water, and which stood no more than a hundred feet off to the east. The mast shifted slightly in a gust of wind, but it had stood for a couple of centuries and showed no sign of collapsing just yet.

"Yeah," he continued, "it's pretty crazy to think of all the boats that sank out here. They reckon there are thousands, and of course a lot of them sank with all hands on deck. Even the lifeboats have to be careful about coming around here." He turned and looked toward the distant shore for a moment, and then he spotted another exposed mast. "Sometimes I find it hard to believe that all this stuff's out here, just a few miles from town. It's almost like we live right next to a massive maritime graveyard. Not that anyone can get down to the treasures, mind. Haven't you heard that old saying? The sands keep what they take."

"Hey, is that one of those shrimp?" Willy asked, dropping to his knees and trying in vain to catch something that had briefly moved in one of the shallow pools of water. "Damn, I think it went into that hole."

"You've got to be careful," Johnny replied, and he knelt at a different pool. "There's an art to this. You two blundering buffoons won't catch anything if you go storming about in those heavy old boots. Don't you remember that I told you to wear something light?"

"Who made you an expert?" Harry asked.

"Watch."

After setting his bucket down, Johnny cupped his hands and gently reached them into one of the pools.

"There's nothing in there, man," Harry pointed out.

"Just watch. I learned from the best."

They all waited, but as the seconds ticked past, Willy and Harry were already starting to get bored. They glanced at one another, and they both rolled their eyes, but then when they looked back at the pool they saw that several tiny creatures were moving closer to Johnny's hands. The creatures were so small, and so nearly transparent, that they were difficult to make out at all.

"Hey," Willy said, "where -"

"Be quiet," Johnny said firmly. "Believe it or not, even the sound of your voice might scare them away. They're jittery little things."

He watched the water, waiting as each shrimp in turn moved closer to his hands, and then – in a sudden movement – he pulled his hands up and moved them quickly over to the bucket. Within seconds, he'd managed to drop each shrimp into captivity, and then he smiled as he looked up at his friends.

"Seriously?" Willy said, raising a skeptical eyebrow. "*That's* what your uncle brought us out here to help with?"

"That bucket now contains enough of those little guys to pay a man's wage for a week," Johnny explained.

"Really?"

Willy and Harry looked down into the bucket for a moment, before turning to one another.

"We're in the wrong line of work," Harry suggested. "Forget hard work in the pits. We should be chasing these little things."

"You guys can pick it up as you go along," Johnny said, already returning his focus to the pool. "If you're smart, that is."

"Okay, so how do *you* know all the tricks?" Harry asked him.

"I used to come out here as a kid."

"With your uncle?"

"Yeah, and -"

Johnny stopped himself just in time. For a fraction of a second, he allowed himself to think back to those idyllic summer afternoons when his uncle would ferry a few of them out to the dunes. They'd hunt in the pools, of course, but as far as Johnny was concerned back then the main point of the trips was always the chance to steal some time with Hazel. The pair of them would spend hours having fun together, learning how to fish in the pools and occasionally playing games in the sand. Even now, twenty years later, Johnny couldn't help but smile as he thought of those innocent days. Back then, he'd been ten and Hazel had been nine, and he'd felt absolutely certain that they'd be together forever.

That was not, however, quite how things had worked out.

"Just get on with it," he muttered, trying to ignore the pang of sadness that he felt in his chest. "You won't have much luck at the start, but with patience you should manage."

He focused on the pool, but less than a minute later he heard Harry let out a labored sigh.

"This is no good," Harry said. "It's as if they don't like me."

"I told you to be patient."

"I was!"

"That was barely a minute ago."

Harry sighed again.

Looking past him, Johnny saw his uncle and a few other men over on the far side of the sandbank, and then he realized that Willy seemed to have wandered off. He turned the other way, and he saw that Willy was walking to one of the sandbanks closer to the water's edge.

"Hey," Johnny called out, "Willy, remember what I told you about the white patches! Whatever you do, don't step on them, okay? Those are the ones that -"

Suddenly Willy let out a cry and fell down, and Johnny immediately scrambled to his feet.

"What's wrong?" Harry asked. "Come on, the guy's an idiot, he only -"

"I told him to be careful!" Johnny shouted, as he began to race across the sandbank. "Willy! What the hell are you doing, man? I told you to stay clear of those patches!"

As soon as he reached Willy, he saw that his worst fears had been realized. The man had vanished, leaving only a churning area of stark white sand. After a couple of seconds, Johnny saw the tips of a couple of fingers reach up; he tried to grab the fingers, but they sank too quickly, and already more sand was rushing down to fill the hole that had swallowed Willy completely.

"Man down!" Johnny yelled, taking care not to get dragged into the sand himself as he leaned forward and reached down. "Get a rope! We've got a man in a sinker!"

He desperately tried to find Willy, but there was no sign of him at all. A moment later, the other men from the boat rushed over with a couple of ropes, but already Johnny was starting to worry that they were too late.

"This is a joke, right?" Harry asked nervously as he reached them. "He's messing with us. Right?"

Grabbing a piece of wood attached to one of the ropes, Johnny began to wedge it down into the sand.

"Hopefully he can grab hold of this," he explained. "It's his only chance right now, otherwise the sand'll drag him down and he'll never be seen again."

"Bloody idiots!" his uncle snapped. "I knew I should never have let you lot come out with us today! The sands aren't for playing on! They're dangerous!"

"I know that!" Johnny snapped, as he desperately waited for some sign that Willy had managed to grab the wooden post in the depths. "I told him to be careful! Why didn't he listen? Why don't people ever listen?"

CHAPTER TWELVE

Twenty years earlier...

"WHY DON'T YOU EVER listen?" Hazel asked as she brushed some more wet sand from the side of Johnny's trousers. "Look, now you're all wet!"

Smiling, Johnny turned and looked over his shoulder. On the far side of the sandbank, his uncle and all the older men were still trying to catch the specimens that were gathered in the various pools of water. Turning back to Hazel, Johnny was already starting to think that it would be fun to really splash her. He was only ten years old, and Hazel was a year younger, and they were starting to spend almost all their spare time together. His friends at school had told him that he couldn't have a girl as a best friend, but Johnny was starting to think that they might be wrong.

"Let me show you again," she said, as she reached her hands back down into the nearest pool of water.

"You already showed me," he replied.

"And you didn't learn!"

She dipped her hands beneath the surface and waited.

"Nothing's happening," Johnny pointed out.

"You have to be patient."

"Being patient is boring," he complained.

"Just try it with me," she said, looking over at him.

"Fine." He dipped his hands into a different pool and waited, although he was already fairly certain that nothing was going to happen. Still, he didn't want to push Hazel *too* far, so he figured he'd play along. "I'd better catch a nice big, juicy shrimp," he continued. "I don't want a little one."

"It's the little ones that are tastiest," she told him. "That's the whole reason we're out here. The other ones are easy to catch." She glanced at him and smiled. "You'll see. I'm right and you know it."

Choosing not to argue with her, Johnny focused on watching the pool. So far, he'd seen no signs of life, but a few seconds later he heard a splashing sound and turned to see that Hazel was already dropping something into a bucket.

"See?" she said. "I got five already!"

"You're cheating. There aren't any in this pool."

"They don't stay in one pool," she explained. "You have to lure them in by being really still, and then you scoop them out. You just have to be -"

"Patient, I know," he said with a sigh, as he looked around to see if any other pools might be more promising. "I've tried being patient and it isn't working. There's no -"

Stopping suddenly, he saw that something small and seemingly metallic was glinting in the sunlight as it poked out from the sand. He squinted to try to get a better look, and then he got to his feet and hurried over, trampling in the pool of water as he went.

"Where are you going?" Hazel called out.

"I saw something," he replied, kneeling down and starting to dig the item out from the sand. "There's something here!"

"You're never going to catch anything if you keep getting distracted by shiny stuff," she pointed out.

"You don't know what you're talking about."

Finding that the object, which was about the size of an egg, seemed to be firmly embedded in the sand, he had to work hard to pull it free. Finally, after a little more work, he held the item up and wiped sand from its sides, and he saw that it was a very old-looking metal sphere with several cuts and dents on its sides. He was a little disappointed, although he quickly realized that the sphere might yet prove to be useful.

"I got you something," he said, as he crawled back over to Hazel and held the sphere out for her to see. "Look!"

"What is it?" she asked.

"I don't know. Something from a shipwreck, I suppose."

"I don't think we should take it," she told him. "You should put it back where you found it."

"No way!" He wiped some more sand away. "Fine. If you don't want it, then I'll keep it for myself. I'm sure it's worth something, whatever it is. I bet it's worth more than some stupid shrimp, anyway."

***

An hour later, as they sat on the fishing boat and began the journey back to the shore, Hazel and Johnny peered down into the various buckets and saw the day's catch.

"It's not a lot," Johnny pointed out.

"It's enough," she replied, as she watched one particular shrimp bump against the bucket's side. "I almost feel sorry for them. They don't even know that they're worth so much. Imagine being so valuable and never going it." She paused. "Imagine being so valuable, and all it does is get you eaten!"

"The whole thing's stupid," Johnny said, sitting back and starting to take another look at the metal sphere that he'd found embedded in the mud. "This is way more interesting than some dumb shrimp. It probably came off a big treasure boat, maybe it once belonged to pirates. Or it might be from some war. There are so many possibilities."

He turned the sphere around in his hands for a moment, before looking over at Hazel. She was still looking into the bucket, and he couldn't understand why *that* was more interesting than the genuine mystery he'd discovered. He desperately wanted Hazel to be impressed, to think that he was really smart for having found the one valuable thing on the entire sandbank, but so far that plan wasn't working at all. For some reason, Hazel seemed far more interested in a pot of wriggling creatures than in a piece of actual treasure.

"Hey," he said, hoping to finally draw her away from the buckets.

He waited.

No reply.

"Hazel."

"They're so cute," she said, still peering down into the buckets. "Come and look at them."

"I don't want to. I've already seen them."

"But Johnny, they -"

"I told you, they're stupid!"

With that, before he could stop himself, he reached out and kicked one of the buckets, knocking it over and sending its contents spilling out across the deck.

"What the hell are you doing, boy?" his uncle yelled, hurrying over and grabbing him by the collar, and then shoving him to the floor.

The metal sphere fell from his hand and rolled away.

Dropping down, his uncle and Hazel began to scoop up as much of the lost catch as possible. Johnny watched, fully aware that he shouldn't have knocked the bucket over but also still furious that he'd been ignored. In fact, he was *still* being ignored, although he knew that he was in trouble. Finally, he decided that he should try to make amends by helping with the clean-up, but a moment later he spotted movement nearby, and he turned to see that his uncle had picked up the metal sphere.

"That's mine!" he said, reaching out to grab the sphere.

"Where did you get this, boy?" his uncle asked.

"I found it. That means it's mine!"

"*Where* did you find it?"

"He found it in the sand," Hazel said. "It was almost buried."

"Don't you know you can't take things from

the sands?" his uncle asked, visibly concerned, before turning and throwing the sphere over the boat's side and into the water.

"No!" Johnny yelled, rushing over to see if there was any chance of getting it back. When he looked down into the sea, however, he realized that he was too late. "That was mine," he whimpered helplessly. "It was treasure..."

"How many times do you children have to be told this?" his uncle asked. "There are rules, especially when you're out at sea. The sands are a special place, and we all know that we shouldn't take anything we find there. Apart from fishing, we leave the sands well alone. Anything they claim from our world, even boats, even people, even stuff that seems like rubbish... All of those things, once they belong to the sands, are gone forever."

"It was only one stupid ball!" Johnny snapped, with tears in his eyes.

"That doesn't matter," his uncle said firmly. "We have to respect the sands. These waters are full of the graves of men who didn't do that, and who paid the ultimate price. The sands are valuable to us, but they don't *belong* to us. We do our best to keep them safe, and part of that means that we don't steal from them. I thought you knew all of this stuff. Maybe you were too young to come out here today after all."

"I'm not too young!" Johnny shouted, but he

knew he was being made to look like a fool in front of Hazel. He turned to her, and then he looked the other way, so that she wouldn't see his tears.

"Just sit down and don't cause any more trouble," his uncle continued, clearly annoyed. "Stupid kids, ruining everything. I won't be bringing you out here again, not until you've grown up a little."

Slumping down, Johnny began to sulk. Hazel sat next to him, but he pulled away when she put a hand on his arm. He felt utterly humiliated, and the last thing he wanted was for her to rub it in. He just wanted to shrink away so that he couldn't be seen, and he wanted to find some way to prove that his uncle had been wrong to treat him so badly. More than anything, he wanted to make sure that he never, ever had to go anywhere near the stupid sandbanks ever again.

CHAPTER THIRTEEN

1955...

"WILLY! WILLY, CAN YOU hear me?"

Still kneeling next to the patch of white sand, still pushing the piece of wood deep in the hope that his friend would grab hold, Johnny waited. At least a minute and a half had now passed since Willy had been sucked beneath the surface. As a cool breeze blew across the sandbank, Johnny realized that any sense of hope was rapidly fading away. He watched the sand for even the slightest hint of movement.

"Where is he?" Harry asked. "Johnny? Where did he go?"

For a moment, Johnny had no idea how to respond. He simply stared at the sand and tried to contemplate the fact that his friend was gone.

"He, uh..."

His lips felt dry.

He turned to Harry.

"He -"

Suddenly they all heard a coughing, spluttering sound coming from a little way off. Turning, they saw that a patch of sand was churning, and a moment later they saw two hands reaching up.

"What the -"

Stumbling to his feet, Johnny raced over and grabbed one of the hands, and Harry did the same. Together, they pulled as hard as they could manage, and finally – miraculously – Willy emerged from the sand, spitting out sand and desperately trying to get big gulps of air into his lungs.

"We thought you were a goner!" Harry shouted.

"How the hell did that work?" Johnny asked, looking back at the spot where Willy had vanished and then at the spot where he'd appeared. "How did you get here, from over there? That's more than ten feet!"

"The sands have natural channels," his uncle muttered, "but still, I've never seen them spit someone out like that before." He patted Willy hard on the back. "Looks like you gave them indigestion, boy!"

"What happened down there?" Johnny stammered, still trying to get his head around the fact that his friend had suddenly reappeared.

"I don't know," Willy gasped, barely able to get the words out. "It sucked me down so fast, man, and then everything went black. I was trying to crawl out, but after a few seconds I didn't even know which way was up anymore. I was trying to breathe, but -"

He started coughing, bringing up more sand in the process.

"I started to swallow this goddamn stuff," he continued. "I don't mind admitting it to you guys, I thought I was a goner down there. And then, suddenly, I realized I could feel cold air on my left hand. That's when I somehow managed to dig myself out. It's like the sandbank pulled me under, shook me around for a while, and then spat me back out."

"That doesn't make a whole lot of sense," Johnny's uncle pointed out. "Most things, once they're down there, they *stay* down there."

"I'm sure glad I didn't," Willy replied. "It was so cold and wet down there. It was horrible, man. That's no place to die."

"Well, you made it," Johnny's uncle continued. "Somehow. It's a million to one shot." He turned to Johnny. "I need to remember not to bring you out here again, boy. The way I see it, every time you're on the sands, some damn foolish thing happens."

"That's fine by me," Johnny told him. "I don't like it out here." He turned and looked across the sandbank. "I never really did."

***

By the time the boat got back to shore, nobody was really much in the mood for talking. Willy had barely said a word since the accident, while Johnny was struck by a strange sense of unease. Harry, meanwhile, was simply bored, and had resorted to picking at the boat's railing.

"I've gotta get home," Willy said, still a little shaky as he finally set foot on dry land again. He stumbled a little on the pebbles. "I don't think I'm ever going back out there. Not me. I'm gonna be a landlubber from now on. You won't see me out there on the sea again."

Kneeling down, he kissed the pebbles, and then he winced slightly as he got back to his feet.

"Are you sure you're feeling okay?" Johnny asked. "I can go with you to see Doctor Ford, if you like."

"No, I'll be fine." Willy took a deep breath, and then he managed a smile. "I cheated death today, huh? It's not everyone that can claim they ever did that. I'm not gonna waste it, though. I swear to you, from this day forth, that I – William George Bailey – am going to live a good and useful life. Maybe I'll run for mayor some day, or I might even try to get elected as an M.P. Or I could start a charity. There are so many possibilities, but I swear I'm not going to waste one more second of my life now that I've had this miraculous recovery!"

As he made his way back into town, he was still muttering away to himself. Harry hurried after him.

"I hope that boy knows how lucky he is," Johnny's uncle said as he wandered over. "I've never heard of a man getting sucked down before and making it back out alive. I can only think that he must've got caught up in one of the currents below the surface."

"Is that even a thing?" Johnny asked.

"I don't know exactly how it works, but it's the only idea that makes even the slightest bit of sense. Still, it goes to show why amateurs and idiots shouldn't ever go out to those sands. They're dangerous at the best of times, even for those of us who know what we're doing. One wrong step and you're dead. Ordinarily, at least."

"Thanks for taking us out there today," Johnny replied, as his uncle traipsed back to the boat.

"Didn't do me much good, did it?" his uncle said, turning and handing him some money. "Share that with your pals. I'll have to go back out there tomorrow and try to top up the catch. And don't even ask to come, because there's not a chance in the whole world I'm ever taking you there again."

"Fine by me," Johnny muttered, as he pocketed the cash. He turned and made his way across the pebbles, heading past all the winches and other fishing gear before reaching the promenade.

"Johnny!"

Turning, Johnny saw a scruffy-looking figure hurrying across Beach Street. Furrowing his brow, he tried to figure out who the man might be, but he was fairly sure that he'd never seen him before in his life. Even as the man got closer, and as Johnny began to notice the ripe smell of body odor and stale beer, he couldn't help but think that there had been a case of mistaken identity. The man looked like a hobo, with a dirty, matted white beard and long, straggly hair poking out from under a large, shabby hat.

"Johnny, we need to talk," the man said, his gruff voice sounding old and tired.

"I'm sorry," Johnny replied, taking a step back, "but I think you've got the wrong person."

"I've been looking for you all morning!"

"I don't know who you -"

"It's me!" the man exclaimed, before removing the hat, which didn't help much. "Your mother told me I'd find you here!"

"Who are you?" Johnny asked, and then – in an instant – he realized that he just about recognized the man's eyes after all. "Captain Manners?" he continued cautiously. He'd heard that the man had become a drunken bum, but he still hadn't been prepared for such an awful sight. And smell. "Is that you?"

"We need to talk," Manners replied. "It's about what happened five years ago."

"I really don't think that I -"

"I saw them last night," he continued. "Lund, and the other two dead men. They came to me!"

"And how much had you drunk by that point?"

"It wasn't the drink that brought them," he explained. "I know that, as sure as I know that I'm here right now. Lund and the others came to me with a warning. They told me that if they don't get what they want, the whole town will suffer. They said it's been five years now and we should have delivered him to them, and that now we're out of time!"

"Calm down," Johnny replied. "You've clearly been drinking, and I'm sure this'll all feel a lot better once you've sobered up. *If* you sober up."

"But -"

"None of this even makes any sense," he added. "Lund and the others are dead. I know that's awful, and it's tragic, and we weren't quick enough to save them. But pretending otherwise isn't going to change anything."

"They want him, Johnny! I don't think they're going to stop until they get him!"

"Who?"

"Who do you think?" Manners asked, exasperated. "They want that bastard we pulled from the sea five years ago! They want Edward Smith!"

CHAPTER FOURTEEN

"WHY DO YOU THINK Walter Warden will know anything?" Johnny asked, struggling to remain patient as he followed Manners toward the rectory.

"I told you, Lund mentioned him, he said Warden was the one who wasted the first chance. And Walter was the other man out there that night, remember? It was you, me, and him on that boat."

"Of course I remember. I just don't see that it's relevant."

"They want that Edward Smith fellow," Manners continued, stopping at the rectory's front door and banging the knocker as loud as he could manage. "From the way they were talking last night, it's like they blame us for taking him away from them. What if they reckon we're the ones who have to put things right?"

"How much did you have to drink last night?" Johnny replied, and he was starting to think that he'd humored the old man enough. He'd been hoping that Father Warden would calm the situation down a little. "Listen, I've got better things to do today than run around chasing after ghost stories."

"Oh yeah? Like what?"

Johnny thought for a moment.

"Well, that's my business," he said finally, as Manners knocked again. "I think I'm going to head off, okay? If you want to believe in all this crap, then that's your business, but some of us don't happen to think that ghosts are real."

"Are you looking for Father Warden?"

They both turned, as Edith Peale emerged from the church and made her way across the street to join them.

"I'm afraid I haven't been able to track him down all morning," she continued, wringing her hands with worry. "It's not like him to sleep in, but he hasn't answered my knocks or calls all morning. He was supposed to meet me quite early to go through some of the hymn books. As far as I can tell, he hasn't gone out. You don't think anything's the matter, do you?"

"Of course not," Johnny said, hoping to reassure her, but a moment later he heard a rustling sound. Turning, he saw that Manners had pushed open the side gate and was heading around the side of the building. "Hey!" he yelled. "I'm not sure you should be doing that!"

Sighing, he hurried after the old man, meaning to grab him by the scruff of the neck and pull him out of the rectory's garden. The side path turned out to be overgrown, and Johnny had to duck down to avoid overhanging plants as he finally caught up to Manners, who was peering through one of the windows.

"This has gone on long enough," Johnny said firmly. "Captain Manners, I hate to say this, but you're -"

"He's dead," Manners said suddenly.

"I'm sorry?"

Stepping back from the window, Manners gestured for him to take a look.

"See for yourself," he said, and now all the color had drained from his face. "He's dead, and it doesn't look like it was very peaceful, either."

Telling himself that Manners was imagining things, Johnny cupped his hands around his eyes as he peered through into the rectory. Immediately, however, he saw a body resting on the floor, and he felt a shudder pass through his chest as he realized that he could see Father Warden's dead face, split open and bloodied, with fat worms wriggling through the mess of meat.

***

"And it was a ghost that told you to come here?" Constable Skinner said, raising a skeptical eyebrow as he made another note on his pad. He turned to Manners. "That *is* what you just told me, is it not?"

"No, it wasn't a ghost that told me to come here," Manners replied, unable to hide his sense of irritation. He let out a long sigh. "The ghosts, and you'll note the plural there, simply told me that they want someone returned to them, and they mentioned that Father Warden had failed to do that over the past five years. They told me there's not much time now, and that the town'll suffer. Naturally, I thought to come and check on Warden, and that's when I looked through the window and saw..."

His voice trailed off, and then he and Johnny both turned and looked through to the next room. Father Warden's bloated corpse was being examined by Doctor Ford, who was in the process of using a pair of forceps to carefully part the edge of the split that ran down the dead man's face. It was as if Father Warden's body had been filled with dirty seawater until it had finally burst open.

In another room, Edith Peale was gently sobbing.

"Had you and the deceased gentleman been arguing at all?" Constable Skinner asked.

"I didn't kill him!" Manners shot back.

"Nobody accused you of anything. I'm just

trying to establish your connection to him."

"I hadn't seen him for years!" Manners said angrily. "Almost not since that night!"

"And which night would that be, Sir?"

"You know which night," Manners continued. "The three of us were the only ones on that lifeboat, on the night the *Mercy Belle* went down. There should have been more hands on the deck, but time was critical and we decided we had to launch with what we had. It was me and Warden and Johnny Eggars here, we were the ones who went out there to try to save the *Mercy Belle*. We're the ones who failed those men!"

Pushing past Johnny, he made his way to the sideboard and began to pour himself a drink from Father Warden's selection of bottles.

"I'm not sure that those belong to you, Sir," Constable Skinner pointed out.

"Do you really think Father Warden'll be needing his brandy now?"

With trembling hands, Manners downed a large glass and began to pour himself another.

"If you want to arrest me," he continued, "then arrest me, but you'll have a hard time persuading the owner to press charges."

"Indeed." Constable Skinner made some more notes. "And how exactly do you think that's relevant to what has happened here?" He glanced at Johnny. "And exactly why are *you* here, Sir?" he asked. "Did you receive a ghostly visitation in the night as well?"

"I brought him!" Manners snapped. "You need to watch your tone, young man! Don't you be making fun of me! I was out on those boats before you were even born!"

He downed his second glass of brandy and began to pour a third.

"He brought me," Johnny said, hoping to calm the situation down a little. "Listen, Bobby, I don't exactly know what's going on here, but -"

"It's Constable Skinner, to you. You can only call me Bobby when I'm not on duty."

"Fine, Constable Skinner." Johnny sighed. "I don't know what happened to Father Warden. Finding out is your job, but I'm sure you can tell that neither of us had anything to do with it. Edith Peale didn't have anything to do with it, either." He looked again toward Father Warden's body, as Doctor Ford continued his examination. "I've never seen anything like it, to be honest," he added. "It almost looks unreal."

"It's very much real," Constable Skinner replied, "and I can assure you that we're going to get to the bottom of it. I don't suppose I've got any more questions for the pair of you, but I might need to take another statement at some point. I don't want either of you to leave town in the near future."

"Leave town?" Manners exclaimed. "Where

the bloody hell do you think I'd be going, man?"

"What he means is that we both understand," Johnny added. "We're just as keen as you are to find out what happened here. Do you have any leads at the moment?"

"I'm about to go and speak to Doctor Ford," Constable Skinner said, "but to be honest, I'm as much in the dark as anyone. When I arrived and saw the body..." He paused for a moment. "I've never encountered anything like it. I don't think anyone has. Not around these parts, at least."

"It was the ghosts," Manners said. "I don't know why the pair of you are being so blind about this. The ghosts gave him a chance, then they killed him, and I reckon I'm next on their list if they don't get what they want!" He sighed. "Then again, I suppose you'll all be glad of that, won't you? You'll be happy to see the back of me!"

"We should go now," Johnny muttered, as he tried to lead Manners to the back door. "You know where to find us if you need us, Bobby. Sorry, I meant... Constable Skinner."

"The ghosts killed him!" Manners spluttered, before downing his third glass. "You can't deny the truth!"

"This way," Johnny continued, leading him back outside. "Come on, we need to let them do their job. There's nothing we can do to help Walter Warden now."

AMY CROSS

CHAPTER FIFTEEN

THE CLOCK ON THE town hall struck twelve as Johnny and Manners reached one of the benches, at which point Manners immediately slumped down and looked for a moment as he if might be about to fall asleep.

"This is crazy," Johnny muttered, as he took a seat next to the old man. "I can't believe the state of poor Father Warden. I saw him last night, when he was giving his speech at the memorial. He looked fine. Now he's dead."

"Murdered," Manners grumbled. "By those ghosts."

Johnny turned to him.

"I know it," Manners continued, "even if you won't believe it yet."

"I noticed *you* didn't show up last night,"

Johnny pointed out. He looked over at the spot where, the previous night, a crowd had gathered to mark the anniversary. The stage had been cleared away now. "I suppose I didn't really expect you to, though. I haven't seen you around town for a long time. No-one has. You look..."

He paused as he tried to think of a polite word that wouldn't be an obvious lie.

"I've been drinking myself to death for five years," Manners said, before clearing his throat. "I look like an autopsy waiting to happen. We both know that."

"It wasn't our fault," Johnny said. "What happened to the *Mercy Belle*, I mean. We went out there as fast as we could, but nobody could have got there in time. The boat was completely destroyed. Believe me, I did a lot of soul-searching in the days and weeks after the tragedy, but I honestly don't see what we could have done differently."

"We could have done *something*!"

"Like what?"

"I don't know!" Manners yelled, erupting with anger for a moment before leaning back and letting out a long, heavy sigh. A few passersby had noticed his outburst. "I don't know what we could have done, okay?" he continued. "But we were on duty that night, we were supposed to keep people safe, and we failed. I'm not interested in hearing a load of excuses."

They sat in silence for a moment. Johnny watched a woman emerging from a nearby shop, and he couldn't help but feel jealous of her normal life. That was all he'd ever wanted: a nice, simple, ordinary life with a wife and some children. If he was being honest with himself, in his mind's eye that wife had always been Hazel, and there was nobody else in town who remotely measured up to her.

Not that he was *often* honest with himself, at least not on that subject.

"Last night," Manners said finally, "I saw the ghosts of Captain John Lund, and his two shipmates Percy Weaver and Keith Simmons. They were good men, I knew them well, and last night they came to my house and they told me that we have to deliver that Smith fellow to them. They didn't tell me why, and I don't feel like I want to know. There are mysteries out there, boy. The sea is home to a fair few things that we don't understand, and sometimes I think we're better off just respecting them and giving them what they want. They don't ask for much. This time, it's pretty clear how we can satisfy them. They want Edward Smith, and nothing else will be enough."

"So what are we supposed to do?" Johnny asked. "Slip him into a pair of swimming trunks and tell him to swim out to sea until a ghost turns up and grabs him?"

Exasperated, Manners shook his head.

"Then what?" Johnny continued. "If these ghosts want him – and I'm not necessarily saying for one moment that I believe they even exist – but if they genuinely want him, then what's stopping them from going and getting him? Can't they figure out where he lives?"

"There's a contract between the town and the sea. We have to willingly -"

"That's nonsense!" Johnny added, cutting him off. "You never used to talk like this. All that time sitting around in your living room, drinking whiskey all day, has completely ruined your head. You're ranting like those old-timers we used to make fun of back in the day."

"I *am* one of those old-timers!" Manners snapped. "At least, I am now. You might not want to accept it, boy, but the sea wants Edward Smith, and the sea isn't used to being denied. If we don't deliver him willingly, on behalf of the town, then I dread to think what'll happen to Crowford."

Johnny hesitated, trying to make sense of everything he'd heard, and then finally he got to his feet.

"This is as far as I go," he told Manners, as he took a step back. "I don't have time in my life to get involved in some drunk old man's wild fantasies, and I'm certainly not going to kidnap a man and toss him into the sea just because of some stupid superstition. It was nice seeing you again, we should meet up *every* five years."

"I'll be dead in five years."

"So haunt me," Johnny said as he turned and walked away.

"What have you got to do that's so important, eh?" Manners called after him, before slumping back in the bench and letting out a long sigh. He still wasn't quite used to being outside during the day, and the sunlight made him squint as he watched people wandering in and out of the shops. "The sea gets what it wants," he muttered under his breath. "Better for us to give it willingly, than to have it wrenched out of our hands."

***

As he made his way along Beach Street, heading home for a nap, Johnny couldn't help but feel sorry for Manners. Whereas once Captain Manners of the *James Furnham* had been one of the town's most loved and respected figures, now the man was nothing more than a drunk, parroting the most ludicrous ideas. The morning's experience was almost enough to make Johnny want to swear off alcohol for good.

Almost.

Besides, he he'd meant what he'd told Manners. The trip out to the sands meant that he had some money in his pocket, but he had to share it with Harry and Willy, and he was sick of just picking up little jobs here and there. He wanted a proper, steady income, but at the same time he wasn't quite ready to join so many others of his generation and go down into the coalmines. He needed a better plan.

Reaching the roundabout, he was about to head down St. Dunstan Street when he saw that a small crowd had gathered at the entrance to the pier. Johnny had lived in Crowford his whole life, and he could tell that this crowd wasn't part of some organized event, so he changed direction and wandered over to investigate. As he got closer to the crowd, he realized he could hear concerned voices calling out, and a moment later there was a loud bang, as if some part of the pier's structure had collapsed.

"What's going on?" Johnny asked.

Bill Burnside turned to him.

"One of the walkways has started to come apart," he explained. "Apparently there's a whole lot of rust on the underside. The chap who oversees the pier swears it wasn't like that yesterday, but that amount of rust can't just show up overnight. He's got some explaining to do."

"The pier's not even thirty years old," Johnny pointed out. "There's no way it should be falling apart already."

"Which is why there are going to be some questions about the upkeep," Burnside said. "The man gets paid a fair wage to look after the pier. How's he let it get into this state?"

Spotting some other men jumping over the railing and rushing down the beach to help, Johnny figured that he might as well join them. He pushed past the edge of the crowd and hopped down onto the pebbles, and then he hurried down the steep slope that led to the underside of the pier entrance. Looking up, he immediately saw that several of the pier supports were encrusted in a kind of heavy rust that appeared to have spread up overnight from the water. At that moment, as if to underline the damage, another chunk of the walkway fell down, causing some of the other men to scatter in an attempt to keep from getting hit.

"Careful!" Charles Barnchester shouted. As the man who was in charge of the pier, he now had the job of forcing some of the men back. "It's not safe to be too close!"

"This wasn't like this earlier," Johnny said, as he recalled setting out on the fishing boat at the crack of dawn. They'd gone close to the pier, and he was certain he'd have spotted so much damage.

"It can't have sprung up overnight," a man nearby replied.

"I know, but I swear this wasn't..."

As his voice trailed off, Johnny looked at

the pier supports, and he couldn't help but notice once again that the rust appeared to have spread up from the surface of the water, like fingers reaching from the sea to the walkway. His first thought was that the rust seemed to have taken the shape almost of a hand, grasping out from beneath the waves to grab at the pier itself. He tried to put that image out of his mind, although it lingered for a moment and he couldn't shake a faint sense of concern.

"The pier's going to have to be closed for the foreseeable future," Charles Barnchester called out to everyone, "and no-one can come down here, either. I won't be held responsible if there's damage from falling sections. I'm going to have to call someone in from out of town to undertake a full survey of the structure."

Still not quite able to believe what he was seeing, Johnny turned to walk away, only to spot a familiar figure up on the promenade. Manners had arrived to see what all the fuss was about, and for a moment the two men's gazes met. Quickly realizing that he didn't want to get caught up in any more nonsense, however, Johnny turned and hurried away in the other direction. He told himself that any trouble with the pier was simply caused by years of neglect, and that he must have missed the damage earlier. He certainly wasn't going to listen to Manners again, or even contemplate the absurd possibility that this development had anything to do with Edward Smith.

The last thing he wanted was to end up like Captain Manners, spouting ridiculous superstitious nonsense and talking about the sea as if it somehow wanted revenge.

AMY CROSS

CHAPTER SIXTEEN

"EDWARD!" HAZEL SHOUTED, shaking her husband's shoulder again. "Edward, you're having a nightmare! Wake up!"

Startled, Edward suddenly opened his eyes and let out a gasp. For a moment, he was trapped between a dream and the waking world. Staring up at his wife, he couldn't quite understand why she was suddenly leaning over him, but then he realized that he was in bed, and he remembered that he'd decided to take a nap after working all morning. Sitting up, he felt his vest clinging to his chest, and when he looked down he saw that he was absolutely drenched in sweat.

"You were shouting," Hazel continued, clearly troubled as she sat next to him on the bed. "I was worried you were going to wake Tobias. What were you dreaming about?"

"I..."

He tried to remember, but although he could still feel the sensations – fear, and horror, and some kind of panic – he was unable to work out exactly what had been happening in the nightmare. He took a slow, deep breath in an attempt to calm his racing heart, but already the nightmare was slipping even further from his thoughts, although for some reason he felt certain that he'd been in darkness, and that the ground beneath his feet had been moving.

"I don't know," he said finally, forcing a smile. "It's over now."

"You seemed to have the fear of God in you," she told him, as she put the back of her hand against his forehead. "You're quite warm, Edward."

"It's nothing."

"I'd like to -"

"I said it's nothing!" he snapped, pushing her hand away, before immediately relenting. "I'm sorry," he added, "I just..."

His voice trailed off as, in an instant, he realized that he remembered at least one part of the nightmare. He waited, hoping that more would come, but deep down he was troubled by a deeper certainty: somehow, he knew that the nightmare had not been *just* a nightmare. It had been a memory, or a fraction of a memory at least; something to go along with the voice he'd heard the day before. Was it really possible that he was staring to remember that awful night five years ago, when the *Mercy Belle* had gone down?

"How about a nice cup of tea?" Hazel asked. "That always makes things seem better."

"Thank you," he murmured, and then he realized that she was waiting for him to get up. "Why don't you go and put the kettle on," he continued, "and I'll be down in a moment?"

"Of course."

Getting to her feet, she seemed a little hesitant, but finally she headed to the door. She glanced back at him and offered a faint smile, and then she made her way onto the landing and down the stairs.

Left alone, Edward felt a shudder pass through his bones as he thought of the terrifyingly real nightmare that he'd experienced. Contrary to the sense of confusion he'd felt upon waking, he was now starting to remember more and more of that horrific night, and he was convinced that it was through his dreams that these memories were starting to seep back into his consciousness. Why they were doing so now, he could not possibly imagine, but each time he blinked he found that he could see more and more of the *Mercy Belle*'s deck on that fateful night, until finally he even remembered the sensation of wind and rain blowing against his face.

"What the hell are you doing here?" Captain Lund had yelled at him, as the boat had almost tipped over in the raging storm.

"Are you insane?" Percy Weaver had asked, rushing over to him and grabbing him by the shoulders. "You could have been killed!"

"I..."

He remembered feeling utterly confused, but he still had no idea how he'd ended up on the boat. A moment later, however, he remembered the *Mercy Belle* getting hit by another huge wave, which had cracked one of the guardrails and sent water washing across the deck.

"We should never have turned around for you," Percy had continued, steadying himself for a moment. "This storm's getting stronger by the second. We'll never make it home!"

"You've doomed us!" Keith Simmons had shouted, with tears in his eyes. "We'll never see the shore again, and it's all your fault!"

"Everyone get back to your stations!" Captain Lund had called out. "We're not giving up yet, not without a fight! I want you all to do your jobs! And as for you -"

Edward remembered Captain Lund turning to him.

"I don't know how in God's name you ended up here," the man had continued, "but you might as well at least be useful. Get in here and help me secure the wheel!"

He remembered rushing over to assist the captain, and he remembered the fear he'd felt at that moment. He'd been confused, and at the same time terrified, but he still was unable to reach back further in his memories, or to understand how he'd ended up with those other men on the deck of the *Mercy Belle*. Even as he recalled the moment when he'd tried to help Captain Lund turn the wheel, he found himself wondering whether he'd genuinely caused the tragedy that had struck the boat that night.

"I'm sorry," he remembered telling Captain Lund. "Please, you have to believe me, I don't understand what's happening."

"A likely story," the captain had replied. "When we get to dry land, man, you'll have some explaining to do, starting with -"

Suddenly they'd both heard a cry, and they'd turned just as the boat had smashed against another huge wave. This time, part of the hull had cracked open, and water had rushed onto the deck with such force that Keith Simmons had been washed away before their very eyes. The man had screamed, but his scream had been cut short by the terrible sound of another wave crashing into the boat and smashing another part of the hull.

"Grab him!" Captain Lund had shouted, but it had already been already too late.

Simmons was gone.

"I don't see him!" Percy had shouted, rushing over to the other side of the boat and trying to spot the missing man in the water. "Keith! Can you hear me?"

"No man could survive being down there," Captain Lund had said firmly. "We've lost him. May the Lord have mercy on his soul, and may his family -"

Before he'd been able to finish, the boat had been struck again, and this time Percy Weaver had been obliterated in the face of a massive wave. Edward remembered seeing the man getting smashed against one of the railings, and he felt a shudder as he remembered the brief site of Percy's back getting snapped in the middle. He thought he might also have seen the man's head splitting away from his body. Then Percy, too, had been gone, and the bow of the *Mercy Belle* had dipped beneath the waves for the final time.

"She's lost," Captain Lund had said, stepping back from the wheel. "There's no hope now."

"That's not true!" Edward remembered shouting, and he'd grabbed the wheel in a desperate attempt to regain some semblance of control. "We can't give up now!"

"I'll never see my Moira again," Captain Lund had continued, as the wrecked boat had begun to lurch to the starboard side. "Or my sons, either. I only hope that they know I loved them, and that I fought to the last to save my vessel. If only I could see them one final time and tell them how much they -"

Another wave had crashed against the boat at that moment, shattering one side and sending both Edward and Captain Lund tumbling into the water. Edward had heard the captain cry out in sheer terror, but that cry had been swiftly silenced by the water, and as Edward grabbed a floating chunk of wood he'd immediately realized that he was the only man left. He'd scrambled up more firmly onto the wood, clinging on for dear life, although a moment later another wave almost sent him tumbling off. And then...

Blinking again, Edward realized he was still sitting on the bed, and that the memory had reached its limit. For now, at least. Still, he'd recalled a great deal, even if he didn't quite understand how he'd ended up on the *Mercy Belle*, or where he'd come from. Those secrets remained just out of reach, although he was more certain than ever that they must be hidden somewhere in his mind.

"Darling?"

He looked over at the doorway and saw that Hazel had come back upstairs, and in that moment he realized he could hear the whistle of the kettle on the stove down in the kitchen.

"Are you sure you're alright?" she asked.

"I'm fine," he stammered, figuring that there was no point telling her about the memories. Not yet, anyway. Not while so many questions remained. "I was just being a little slow, that's all." He clambered out of bed. "Now, how about we get that tea?"

She smiled, and Edward told himself that there was no point forcing the rest of the memories to come back. Evidently they were still there, and they would reveal themselves in time. In truth, as he followed his wife downstairs, there was now a part of him that didn't *want* to remember. After all, he had a good life now. What if, by remembering, he put that life in jeopardy? Would it really be so bad if things just stayed the way they were?

CHAPTER SEVENTEEN

THREE WEEKS LATER, as he stepped around the counter in his grocery store and peered into the boxes that Colin Worthington had delivered, Donald Morley felt a flicker of dread in his belly.

"I know what you're thinking," Colin said cautiously, trying to head off any criticism early, "and they might not look like much, but as far as I can tell they're still good enough to eat."

"How am I ever going to get anyone to buy something like this?" Donald asked, holding up a turnip and already feeling that it was soft to the touch. "People have been complaining for a couple of weeks now. I've been buying my produce from your father's farm for as long as I've been in business, Colin, but this stuff... I just can't sell it."

"We've had a bad few weeks, that's all,"

Colin replied. "Dad says things'll turn around soon. We just have to be patient. Besides, the stuff isn't *that* bad. People are going to have to accept what we can offer them."

"You don't know the grocery business," Donald said. "Every year, my customers get pickier and pickier, to the extent that -"

Before he could finish, he felt the turnip starting to shake slightly. Startled, he set it down on the counter and took a step back, just as one side of the vegetable crumbled away and a large black beetle began to crawl out.

"That's a one-off," Colin said uncertainly.

"There were beetles in the bottom of that box of carrots you brought me on Thursday," Donald said with a sigh. "I don't know what you're doing out there at that farm, but I can't accept any of this produce."

"We haven't changed *anything*!" Colin told him. "I swear!"

"Then explain this!"

"I can't! I don't know what's wrong, it's like nothing we do is actually working anymore! The fishermen are having a bad time too, their catches are down to almost nothing." He sighed. "Dad's just as confused as I am. It's almost like..." His voice trailed off for a moment. "If I didn't know better," he continued, "I'd be starting to think that our farm is cursed. It's as if the land itself has turned against us."

Donald cast a skeptical glance at him, but before he could say anything they both heard a cry from outside. Rushing over to the window, Donald looked out and saw that there was a commotion at the front of the town hall. Several people, including some women, appeared to be in distress, so Donald hurried outside and crossed the road, with Colin right behind. As they got closer to the town hall, they saw that a number of chunks of concrete lay smashed on the pavement.

"I was almost hit!" Mavis Purdey was saying, clearly in a state of panic. "It missed me by a matter of inches!"

Looking up, Donald saw that part of the facade of the town hall had collapsed. A moment later, another chunk came loose and crashed down, and everyone in the small crowd immediately stepped a little further back.

"Maybe it's not just our farm," Colin muttered darkly. "I'm starting to think that there's something wrong with the whole bloody town!" He turned to Donald. "Maybe there *is* a curse after all!"

***

"Okay, higher!" Johnny called out, as he stood on the beach and looked up to where Harry was dangling against one of the pier's support beams. "A little higher! Just keep going until I say to stop!"

All around them, work was progressing to fix the damage to the pier. A surveyor had identified several areas where rust had – seemingly overnight – managed to cause serious weakness. Plenty of people had argued that this was impossible, that the pier had been fine until the moment when the first pieces had come loose, but there was no denying the fact that the damage *had* happened. And now it had to be repaired.

As far as Johnny was concerned, the chance to do a few weeks' work was one positive to come out of the situation, and he was earning well enough for what was turning out to be some pretty grueling physical labor.

"There!" he told Harry, just as he spotted Benny Burville also climbing down a rope from the walkway. "Benny, don't get in the way, okay?"

"I won't!" Benny yelled. "I just have to carry out some checks!"

"Can't you wait?" Johnny asked.

"Relax, I know what I'm doing."

Benny lowered himself a little further, and Johnny – who figured that he couldn't be expected to keep an eye on the entire site – returned his attention to Harry.

"Right there!" he yelled. "Okay, you're doing great. Just mark that spot so that the next guys know exactly where they're supposed to put the new hooks."

Putting his hands on his hips, he watched as Harry got to work, and he told himself that so far things were going pretty well. The incessant noise from all the hammering was giving him a slight headache, but he was getting used to that, and he was hoping that he might be able to turn the temporary work into a permanent position with one of the companies that had been drafted in. He'd never really held down a proper, long-term job in Crowford before, and he was sick and tired of always having to duck and dive in his search for work. He'd already decided that, if he was offered a job out of town, he might well take it. After all, there wasn't really anything keeping him in Crowford. Not anymore.

"Okay, now get yourself back up!" he shouted to Harry. "We've still got all that part around the entrance to do before we can even think about taking a lunch break."

He turned to head back up the beach, but at that moment he heard a sudden, ominous snapping sound. Instantly realized that something was wrong, he looked back over his shoulder just as he heard a cry, and he watched in horror as Benny Burville plummeted from a broken rope and smacked headfirst into one of the concrete blocks. A sickening cracking sound rang out, before Benny's body slumped down against the pebbles and slid down toward the shore.

"What the hell?" Johnny shouted, rushing over to check on the injured man.

Dropping to his knees next to the spot where Benny had come to a halt, he reached out and put a hand on his friend's shoulder. For a moment, he was able to believe that Benny might be alright, but then he began to roll him over, only to let out a shocked gasp as soon as he saw that most of the upper half of the man's head had been smashed away, leaving only a pulpy mess with a row of teeth poking out from the bloodied gums. A section of brain was visible deep in the meat, but all of Benny's face and forehead had been destroyed.

Turning, Johnny saw a large bloodied stain all over the edge of the concrete block.

"Is he okay?" Malcolm, the foreman of the site, yelled as he ran over to check, only to stop as soon as he saw the answer for himself. The color instantly drained from his face.

"What happened?" Harry shouted, still dangling from one of the other ropes. "Is he hurt?"

Benny's body shuddered, but as Johnny looked back down at him he realized that the man was simply experiencing some kind of post-death spasms. Sure enough, the body quickly fell still, although blood continued to pour from the remains of his head, spilling out onto the pebbles.

"Everybody get off those ropes!" Malcolm

yelled. "I don't want anyone using them until I know what caused this!"

"It's like it just snapped," Johnny pointed out, as he tried to hold himself together. "It's like the rope just broke for no reason."

Suddenly a woman screamed over on the promenade, and Johnny immediately pulled off his jacket and placed it over Benny's head so that nobody else would see the mangled mess. He quickly saw blood soaking through the jacket's fabric, but he figured that at least his friend – who he'd known since they'd been classmates together at Crowford School – would be afforded a little dignity.

"I want this whole area cleared!" Malcolm shouted. "Do you hear me? Everyone has to stop work right this instant, and get away from the pier!" He turned and looked back down at Benny's body. "I put every safety measure in place, I swear. Those ropes were tested and retested, there's no way one of them should have failed like that." He paused. "Benny had a wife, she's due to give birth in a few months. Now that poor kid's going to grow up without a father."

"You did everything you could," Johnny told him. "Benny's wife will be looked after. Everyone'll rally around her and the kid. We look after each other here in Crowford."

"It was an accident," Malcolm continued.

"That's all. What if people blame *me*? What if they think that his death is my fault?"

"They won't," Johnny said, although he could feel a sense of dread spreading through his chest. "There have been a lot of accidents in Crowford lately. A lot of bad luck." He turned and looked out across the sea. "It's almost as if the town's being punished for something."

CHAPTER EIGHTEEN

"TO BENNY," HARRY SAID, raising his pint across the table. "May he rest in peace."

"To Benny," Willy added.

"To Benny," Johnny said, and the three of them clinked their glasses together. "God bless his soul."

They'd been drinking in the Crowford Hoy all afternoon, even though they weren't really in the mood to get drunk. The pub wasn't even supposed to be open, but blind eyes were often turned in Crowford, especially when a man had died. Work at the pier had been halted and the whole town was in shock, and Johnny in particular just wanted to wipe the awful images of Benny's corpse from his mind. He couldn't help replaying those terrible final moments over and over in his head, and he wasn't sure that he'd ever be able to close his eyes again without seeing Benny's bloodied head.

"Wow," Willy said suddenly, "is that..."

Hearing a bumping sound, Johnny turned and looked across toward the bar, and he felt an immediate thud of irritation as he saw that Captain Manners had stumbled through the door. He told himself that maybe he'd be okay, that Captain Manners wouldn't notice him, but a moment later the old man made his way over. Looking back down at his pint, Johnny reminded himself that he had to stay calm and polite.

"Did you hear?" Manners shouted as he reached the table. He nudged Johnny's shoulder. "It's been getting bad for weeks now, but finally a man died! A man actually lost his life!"

"I know!! James said firmly. "I was there."

"Then you don't need me to tell you what's happening," Manners continued, before nudging him again. "How much more proof do you need?"

"What's this about?" Willy asked. "Johnny, what does he mean?"

"Nothing," Johnny replied, through gritted teeth, before turning to Manners. "Do you mind? Our friend died today, we were at school with him. We really don't want to be interrupted right now, especially not by someone who's peddling ridiculous stories."

"What kind of stories?" Willy asked.

"You don't want to know," Johnny told him.

"I knew this was going to happen," Manners announced, swaying slightly on his feet. "Or something like it, at least. This is what they meant when they said that the town would suffer if we don't turn that bastard over to them! Crops are failing, the boats are barely catching any fish, buildings are literally starting to crumble and now a man is dead!"

"I know!" Johnny yelled, getting to his feet and pushing Manners back with such force that the old man bumped against the wall. "I know he's dead! I saw it happen!"

Realizing that everyone else in the pub had stopped talking, Johnny looked around and saw that he was the center of attention. He considered telling them all to mind their own business, but at the last moment he figured that he'd only end up causing more of a commotion, so he sat down and told himself that hopefully Manners would get the message and leave him alone.

"So what's this about turning someone over to someone?" Willy asked. "I don't get it."

"Don't encourage him," Johnny said. "Please."

"Everything that's happened in this town over the past few weeks is because of him," Manners said. "You remember when Father Walter Warden was found dead? That was the first warning sign."

"They never figured out what happened to him, did they?" Harry said.

"He was killed because he didn't deliver the Smith man to the sea!"

"The Smith man?" Harry paused. "You mean Edward Smith?"

Johnny put his head in his hands.

"The sea wants him," Manners explained. "You can laugh at me if you want, but the sea has a claim on Edward Smith and it won't let that claim go. I don't pretend that I understand all of this, but that's neither here nor there. There are mysteries that man can't comprehend. We have to willingly deliver that man to the sea, so they can do whatever it is to him that they want to do, or Crowford will see no let-up in all this pain and suffering. I haven't seen Lund and the others for a few weeks, but I know they'll be back soon. I'll end up the same way as Warden, and then..."

He looked down at Johnny.

"You'll probably be next, boy," he added. "After all, it was you, me and Warden who saved Smith."

"Do you mean Captain Lund?" Harry asked. "From the lifeboat? The one that sank?"

"I've seen his ghost!" Manners hissed. "And the ghosts of Simmons and Weaver as well! The sea is using them in order to communicate with us. It won't rest until it has what it wants!"

"This is all nonsense," Johnny said with a sigh. He looked over at his friends. "You know not to listen to this old fool, don't you? Believe me, everything he's just told you is just the tip of the iceberg. He has some even more absurd claims to make if you let him."

"I kinda want to hear what he has to say," Willy said cautiously. "Ever since my near-death experience a few weeks ago, I feel like I should be more open to unusual possibilities."

"Edward Smith is going to end up being returned to the sea," Manners said as he took a seat at the end of the table. "That much, I can promise you. If he isn't, this entire town will end up ruined, and nobody's going to be willing to countenance something like that. The only question is *when* we deliver Smith up. The sooner the better, if you ask me, because by delaying the inevitable we're only bringing more pain and misery upon ourselves."

"Benny Burville died because a rope snapped," Johnny said firmly.

"What about the crops?" Harry said. "What about the fishing? What about all the other things that have been going wrong over the past few weeks? Part of the town hall collapsed today!"

"I'm not denying that these things have happened," Johnny said with a sigh, "but none of that means that three ghostly fishermen are here as envoys of the sea, demanding some kind of sacrifice. If you think about it for just a moment, you'll realize how ridiculous the whole idea is."

He waited for them to agree with him.

"So how exactly would he have to be delivered to he sea?" Willy asked Manners. "Would it be enough to just shove him off the end of the pier?"

"Would the whole town have to be involved," Harry added, "or could it be done by, for example, a few men who simply knew what was necessary?"

"As long as he's delivered willingly, it doesn't matter who does it," Manners explained. "I think that's how it works, at least. I'm not entirely sure, the ghosts weren't clear, but I don't think we need Smith himself to be in agreement. If we can somehow get him to the shore, I think the ghosts will take care of the rest. All they need to see is that we're doing the right thing. Or what they consider to be the right thing, at least."

"And why does the sea want him?" Willy asked. "What did he do?"

"We might never know," Manners said. "The man has amnesia and -"

"He *claims* to," Harry replied, interrupting him. "I know some people around town who wonder whether he's faking it. What if he did something really bad, and he's just pretending not to remember?"

"There's absolutely no reason to think that," Johnny said with a sigh. "Don't you think you're all getting a little carried away?"

"If this is the only way to save Crowford," Willy replied, "then I think we have to at least consider the possibility. I don't know, man, I felt something out there on the sandbank when I almost died. I can totally believe that there's some mystical stuff associated with the sea. And you can't deny that Crowford's being going through hard times lately. It genuinely feels at the moment as if the town's cursed."

Staring at him for a moment, Johnny realized that he was serious, that he genuinely seemed to be getting drawn in by everything that Manners was saying. He wanted to grab Willy and Harry and bang their heads together, but after a moment he instead got to his feet.

"Where are you going?" Harry asked.

"I'm getting out of here," he replied. "You guys are talking crazy. I need to clear my head."

"You can't face the truth," Manners told him. "I understand, it's hard, but you'll come around to it sooner or later. You have to."

"We'll see about that," Johnny muttered, turning and hurrying out of the pub, even as the others implored him to stay.

Once he was outside, Johnny leaned back

against the wall and told himself that there was no need to worry. He looked both ways along the street, and he tried to focus on the fact that everything certainly *seemed* normal. Crowford didn't look like a town that was under a curse, and there was also the small matter of Johnny knowing that curses weren't even real. If Harry and Willy wanted to get drunk with old Captain Manners and listen to his spooky stories, that was their problem, but Johnny Eggars had better things to do with his time.

Shoving his hands into his pockets, he set off into town.

CHAPTER NINETEEN

"WE SHOULD NEVER HAVE turned around for you. This storm's getting stronger by the second. We'll never make it home!"

"You've doomed us! We'll never see the shore again, and it's all your fault!"

Standing at the kitchen window, gripping the sides of the sink so hard that his hands were staring to hurt, Edward Smith stared out at the garden and told himself that he had to find a way to ignore the voices in his head. Late afternoon light was casting long shadows across the lawn, and he tried to focus on all the jobs he still had to do, but sure enough a moment later he heard the voices again.

Louder, this time.
More real.

"I don't know how in God's name you ended up here, but you might as well at least be useful. Get in here and help me secure the wheel!"

He gripped the sink even harder. His fingers felt as if they were on the verge of breaking.

And then there was the other sound. Every so often the voices subsided, only to be replaced by the sound of raging waves and smashing wood. He knew this was the sound of the *Mercy Belle* getting destroyed by the storm, and at the same time he swore he could feel the kitchen floor pitching and tilting beneath his feet. It was as if he was on the verge of being fully transported back to that night. It was almost as if the sea was calling to him.

"Edward?"

Now the voices were back, except this time something was different. Why was a woman calling his name? Had there been a woman on the *Mercy Belle* that night?

"Edward."

Suddenly feeling a hand on his arm, Edward spun around and saw that Hazel was standing right behind him. Tobias was out in the hallway, in his pram, and Edward quickly realized that of course there had been no woman on the *Mercy Belle*. He'd just allowed Hazel's voice to mix in with the emerging memories.

"We're going for a walk," she told him cautiously, clearly worried. "Why don't you come with us?"

"No," he replied, before he even knew what he was going to say. "I have a lot to do here."

"It might do you some good."

"I said I'm busy!" he snapped, and then he took a deep breath. "Another time."

"Okay," she said softly, before leaning closer and giving him a peck on the cheek. She hesitated, as if she might be about to say something else, and then she turned and headed through to the hallway.

Edward watched her go.

"I love you," he said suddenly.

She turned back to him.

"And I love *you*," she said. "More than you could ever know. That's why I'm trying to help you. I know something's wrong, and I just wish you'd tell me what it is. If you're starting to remember the -"

"I'm not remembering anything," he replied, interrupting her. "Honestly. I'd tell you if that were the case. I think I'm just not dealing well with the anniversary, that's all. I'll be back to normal in a day or two." He paused, hoping that would be enough, but Hazel was still staring at him. "I promise," he added finally.

"I'm sure it'll be fine," she murmured, before going through to Tobias, who was wriggling in his pram.

"I *will* be fine in a day or two," Edward

whispered under his breath, trying to convince himself even as he heard the surge of the storm once again in his mind. "I have to be."

***

"Daddy's just going through a difficult time," Hazel told Tobias as she pushed him along the darkening street. The pram had a squeaky wheel, which she'd been meaning to get Edward to fix for some time. "There's no need to worry. Everything's going to be perfectly alright."

Even as those words left her lips, she knew that it wasn't really Tobias she was telling. She couldn't shake the feeling that Edward was becoming disturbed in some manner. Although she'd long thought that there might come a day when his memories would resurface, she was worried now that this process was happening in a dangerous, uncontrolled way, and that he might need help. Where that help could possibly come from, she had no idea, but she told herself that as his wife it was her job to find some way to calm his mind.

Stopping on the corner, she crouched down and wiggled the wheel, hoping to fix the incessant squeaking noise. As she did so, however, she heard a scuffing sound coming from over her shoulder, as if somebody else had stopped too. She turned and looked, but all she saw was the gloom of Princes

Street with its terraced houses on either side.

She waited a moment, and then she looked back down at the wheel.

"Daddy has been through a lot, you know," she told Tobias as she fiddled with the wheel. "I suppose one day he'll tell you all about it, or perhaps I'll have to do it, but these past five years have been very difficult for him. I can't even begin to imagine what it's like for anyone to not remember where they come from. He's done so very well, but I can't help thinking that he's standing on foundations that are a little..."

Her voice trailed off as she thought back to the very first moment she'd ever met Edward. She'd been on hand on the night of the *Mercy Belle* disaster, she'd got to Edward even before Doctor Ford had arrived. She'd shone her flashlight down onto Edward's battered face, and she'd seen so much carnage and damage. And then, before she'd had a chance to really do anything, Doctor Ford had reached the scene and taken charge.

In the weeks and months after that night, however, she'd been put in charge of Edward's rehabilitation. That was when they'd really grown closer, and she'd realized quite early on that she couldn't simply abandon him. She knew full well what people in Crowford thought, that she'd simply married him because she pitied a scarred and disfigured man with no memories, with no life or family, but deep down she knew that wasn't true. Deep down, she once again thought back to that moment when she'd first seen his bloodied face, because that had been the moment when some tiny flicker of understanding had ignited in her chest. That had been the moment when -

Suddenly hearing a bumping sound, she got to her feet and once again looked back along Princes Street. There was still no sign of anyone, but she couldn't shake the feeling that she was being watched.

"Hello?" she said cautiously, even though she felt rather foolish by doing so. "Is anyone there?"

She waited, but after a moment she told herself that she was simply imagining things.

"Isn't Mummy a silly old thing?" she asked, turning back to look down at Tobias. She paused again. "One day, the truth about Daddy will come out," she continued. "I know it. When that happens, things might get bumpy for a while, but we'll all be okay so long as we have one another. I feel that here." She touched her chest. "In my heart. He *will* get his memories back." With tears in her eyes, she watched her son for a moment. "And when we get home," she added, forcing a smile, "we really must get Daddy to take a look at this wheel, mustn't we? It's been squeaking for far too long."

With that, she pushed the pram across the

street, and then they began to make their way past the allotments. She glanced down at all the patches that had been marked out, and she quickly saw the patch that belonged to Edward. She'd been so proud of him when he'd started working down there, and she knew that the vegetables were one of the most important things in his life. Sometimes she wondered whether, on one lonely afternoon digging the soil, that might be where Edward would remember everything.

And then what?

If her suspicions about his past were correct, what would happen next?

"Mummy can be a silly old thing sometimes," she told Tobias, hoping to distract herself as she continued to push the pram along the pavement. "Listen to me. Even now, I can't stop -"

Suddenly the ground gave way beneath her feet, as an entire section of the pavement – and the soil beneath – crumbled and fell down the steep slope that led to the allotment. Hazel cried out and tried to grab the railing for support, but the railing had also broken. She and the pram tumbled down the steep slope, and Tobias screamed as he was sent flying from his pram at the bottom. As mother and son landed on the dirty ground, dirt and grass and concrete and broken metal bars rained down all around them.

AMY CROSS

CHAPTER TWENTY

"HAZEL!"

AS HAZEL BEGAN to sit up, she felt someone grabbing her shoulder. She looked up, and through the clouds of dust and dirt she was shocked to see Johnny staring down at her.

"Tobias," she gasped, as she realized she could hear her son crying nearby. "Is he okay?"

Pushing Johnny aside, she scrambled to her feet. She felt a pain in her right ankle, but she ignored that pain completely as she hurried over to where Tobias was crying and wriggling on his back, surrounded by the detritus of the landslide. Scooping her son up into her arms, she sat down on the ground and began to examine the boy for any sign of injury.

"Is he hurt?" Johnny asked, stepping over to

take a closer look.

"Oh, my darling Tobias," Hazel sobbed, still terrified. Her hands were shaking and there were tears in her eyes. "Please, you have to be alright."

Johnny righted the pram, which had survived the fall without any real damage, and then he sat next to Hazel.

"Is he hurt?" he asked again.

"I think he's fine," she said, still filled with a sense of the most profound panic. "I don't see any cuts or bruises."

"Your ankle -"

"Oh, sod my ankle!" she snapped. "I don't care about that right now!"

Johnny looked down at her ankle, which was already a little discolored, and then he glanced back up the slope. The entire section had crumbled away, and as he surveyed the extent of the damage he couldn't help but think that Hazel and Tobias had been lucky. They could both have broken their necks.

"Are you alright down there?" a voice shouted, as a man from one of the nearby houses came into view up on the street.

"The ground gave way!" Johnny told him. "You'd better call the police. The whole area might need sealing off!"

"I've got a phone inside," the man replied. "I'll let them know right now."

"He's fine," Hazel said finally, holding Tobias up as he continued to cry. "Thank you, Lord, for keeping him safe. Oh, thank you so much. I couldn't bear it if anything happened to him."

"He looks pretty healthy," Johnny told her. "I'm more worried about your ankle."

Finally finding a moment to look down at her left foot, Hazel saw that her ankle was indeed injured. She was still in too much shock to really feel the pain, but she knew that would be coming soon. She could tell that the ankle wasn't broken, but there was an almighty bruise and she felt sure that it was – at the very least – badly sprained.

"That doesn't matter," she told Johnny. "All that matters is Tobias."

She paused for a moment.

"What are you doing here?" she asked finally.

"What do you mean? Should I have just walked on by?"

"No, I mean, what are you doing in this part of town at all?" She watched him, and she could see a hint of guilt in his expression as she thought back to the strange sounds she'd heard just a few minutes earlier. "Johnny Eggars," she continued cautiously, "were you following us?"

"No!" he blurted out.

She raised a skeptical eyebrow.

"I was out for a walk," he continued. "To

clear my head. I saw you and the lad, but I didn't want to disturb you."

"Why not?"

"I just didn't. I could have gone a different way, but I was thinking of popping into the Star and Garter for a quiet drink by myself, so I stayed back a little. So I wasn't following you, it was more that I was trying to keep out of your way."

"I can't imagine why you'd do that," she replied. "We're friends, aren't we?"

"Sure we are," he muttered, although he had to look away from her. "There's never been any doubt about that."

They sat in silence for a moment, before Hazel tried to get up. Immediately, she felt excruciating pain in her left ankle, causing her to sit back down.

"Bad, is it?" Johnny asked.

"It'll heal."

"Is it broken?"

She shook her head.

"That's good," he told her.

"I'm going to have to get home," she muttered. "This is terrible, I shall likely be off my feet for days. Weeks, even. Oh, how am I going to get everything done around the house? How am I going to look after Tobias?"

"Your perfect husband'll have to up his game."

She turned and glared at him.

"I didn't mean anything by that," he continued, although he knew he wasn't sounding too convincing. "Honest."

"I don't think it's as bad as it looks," she said, as she once again tried to get up. This time, even though she was still holding her crying son, she managed to stand, although she felt a great deal of pain when she put pressure on her damaged ankle. She took a couple of limping steps toward the pram, and then she set Tobias down among his blankets. "There you go, my darling. There's no need to keep crying. We're both fine, see?"

Johnny watched as she tried to comfort the boy. He was relieved to see that Hazel was okay, because there had been a moment – just after she'd been sent tumbling down the slope – that he'd feared the worst. The thought that she might be hurt, or worse, had been the single greatest moment of horror that he'd ever experienced, but now he felt foolish for having been so worried. After all, she clearly didn't care that much for him, so why was he unable to rid himself of these pesky feelings for her?

"Do you love him?" he asked.

"I'm sorry?"

"That man," he continued, surprised by the bitterness in his own voice, but unable to stop himself. "Edward Smith. Not that Edward Smith is his real name, of course, but it's the one he uses. Do you really love him?"

She took a moment to finish tucking Tobias into his blankets. The boy was finally settling, and after a few seconds his crying became more of a series of gurgles.

"Really, Johnny?" she said tersely, glancing briefly at him before returning her attention to her son. "Are you choosing now, of all times, to ask stupid questions?"

"I -"

"Have you been drinking?"

"Not much."

"I'm not having this conversation with you," she continued. "I refuse. There's absolutely no point."

"If -"

"Thank you for helping us," she added, as she limped around to the other side of the pram, "but we're quite capable of taking care of ourselves from this point onward."

"Don't be bloody silly, woman," he said, getting to his feet and going over to help her. He reached for the pram. "You're hurt. Let me help you get home."

"Absolutely not."

"Hazel -"

"I said no!" she snapped, pushing his hands away from the pram and then pushing him again, this time sending him stumbling back a couple of steps. "What part of that don't you understand?"

"I'm sorry," he said, shocked by her outburst, "I only -"

"I can hear a car in the distance," she continued, "it's probably the police. Would you mind telling them what happened? Obviously I'll be happy to talk to them if necessary, but please ask them not to come to our house tonight. Tell them I'll drop by the station tomorrow and see if there's anything I can help them with."

She turned and began to push the pram away across the uneven ground. She was limping heavily, and after a moment she stopped. She stared down at Tobias, and then slowly she turned to Johnny.

"You asked me whether I love my husband," she reminded him. She paused, trying to work out exactly how to answer that question. "I love that man more than any woman has ever loved a man in the history of the world," she continued finally. "I love that man more than any woman ever *could* love a man. I love him unconditionally, and without hesitation, and I have not felt so much as a flicker of doubt in all the time I have known him. I love him with my whole heart, and I am devoted to him. Our love grows with each passing day, and I will let nothing ever come between us."

"But he's -"

"Do you hear me?" she shouted angrily, before quickly regathering her composure. "I will not have people questioning any of this," she added. "You and any other gossips can think what you like, but I want you to be in no doubt on this matter. I love that man more than life itself. I would die for him. He is more important to me, and more cherished, than all the rest of the world put together. The only exception to that is our son, who is the product of our union, and I adore him with all of my soul. So if you, or anyone else, *ever* think to question my marriage, then you are wasting your time. Edward and I will be together forever."

Johnny paused, letting her words sink in. He'd been prepared for them, but he still found them difficult to accept.

"I suppose that's that, then," he muttered finally, trying to act as if he didn't really care. "You don't need to say more."

"We'll get home under our own steam, thank you very much," she added. "Goodnight, Johnny. Your help has been much appreciated."

With that, she set off again, pushing the pram toward the slope that ran up to the street. She was still limping, but Johnny knew that there was no point going after her and offering again to help. Besides, he figured that she'd be home soon enough, and then that perfect specimen of a man Edward Smith would be able to perform his husbandly duties and take the strain. He knew that it was perhaps wrong of him, but Johnny could already feel a spark of genuine fury starting to burn in his chest. He'd never liked Edward, he'd always resented him for stealing Hazel away, but now something had changed.

Now he really hated the man.

CHAPTER TWENTY-ONE

AS HE MADE HIS way back along yet another of Crowford's streets, with the sun having now dipped below the horizon, Johnny was surprised to find that his rage was not diminishing. In fact, with each step, he could feel himself getting angrier, until he reached the roundabout and saw to his surprise that the a police car was parked a little further ahead.

Stepping out across the road, he realized that there had been some kind of accident. A black car had mounted the pavement and hit a wall, with enough force to crumple its front end. Onlookers had gathered round, although they were being forced to stay at a reasonable distance. Glass and metal had been left strewn across the road, and the closer he got to the scene of the accident, the more Johnny began to realize that the car had suffered serious damage.

"What is it?" he asked as he reached the edge of the crowd. "What's going on?"

"Oh, it's terrible," Mildred Ward told him. "It's Eric Grace. You know, the businessman? He owns half of Crowford!"

"I know who you mean," Johnny said as he watched three police officers pulling a sheet-covered body out of the car. "Is he..."

"He swerved to avoid a sudden hole in the road," Mildred said, as Johnny spotted a section of the road that appeared to have cracked and risen up. "It's so awful, he was such a good man."

"Is he dead?" Johnny asked.

"Killed on impact, they say," she continued. "His poor daughters are going to be so upset. I don't know if anybody has told them yet, but -"

"Daddy!" a voice screamed, and Johnny turned just in time to see Vivian Grace running along the street in her nightdress, with her sister Angela just a short distance behind. "Daddy, where are you?"

For a moment, Johnny could only watch as Vivian dropped to her knees next to the spot where the body had been set down. She tore the sheet away, only to scream as she saw her father's bloodied face. Leaning over him, she began to cling to his lifeless body, as Angela stopped a short way back and stared at the awful scene with an expression of utter shock. Vivian's cries were ringing out through the town.

"Of course, you know who'll inherit the fortune now, don't you?" Mildred whispered. "God help us, because those sisters are going to get everything. Eric Grace was such a good man, he really tried to do what was best for Crowford. I hope his daughters will be the same, and that they won't get too greedy. They're only in their thirties. That's awfully young for so much money and power."

"This town is falling apart," Johnny said, as he looked once again at the damaged road. "The pier. The town hall. The allotments. Everywhere you turn, it's like Crowford is rotting." He paused as he thought of the sight of Hazel and Tobias tumbling down the slope, and he remembered that moment when he'd thought they might be dead. "It can't go on like this," he continued, as Vivian Grace's screams continued to fill the air. "Someone has got to do something."

***

By the time he got back to the Crowford Hoy, Johnny felt more determined than ever. He pushed the door open and stepped inside, and he immediately heard the sound of Willy and Harry talking loudly and animatedly. He stopped for a moment, wondering whether there might be another way, but deep down he knew that he'd already made his decision. Heading to the bar, he bought himself a pint, and then he went through to join the others.

"I was talking to Ernest Dwyer this morning," Captain Manners said, evidently having barely paused in his long diatribe in the hours since Johnny had left earlier. "You might know him, he's something of a local historian. What he doesn't know about Crowford, isn't worth knowing. Anyway, I was asking him about about the sands, and about the sea, and he told me there have always been reports of strange goings on out there. Now, he wouldn't admit to me that he's seen anything himself, but I got the distinct impression that he'd be right on our side."

"But why don't these ghosts just take Edward Smith themselves?" Willy asked. "And why have they waited five years to start pressing their point?"

"I've gone into all of that already," Manners said with a sigh. "Do we really have to go round and round in these circles?" He sighed. "Alright, I'll start at the beginning, and this time I want you all to pay attention. The sea -"

"Johnny!"

As soon as Harry spotted Johnny approaching the table, they all turned to look at him.

"I didn't think you were coming back

tonight," Willy said.

"Yeah, well, plans change," Johnny said as he sat back down in the spot where he'd been a few hours earlier. He took a sip from his pint. "*People change.*"

"Like I was telling you," Manners continued, "the town -"

"Eric Grace is dead," Johnny announced.

The others all turned and stared at him.

"Traffic accident," he continued, looking at each of them in turn. "It only happened about half an hour ago, but it looks like he swerved to avoid a hole in the road. He hit a wall, and he died instantly. It's like the road just started to break apart, and we all know that roads don't usually do that."

"Eric Grace was one of the most important men in the whole of Crowford," Harry pointed out.

"Exactly," Johnny said. "It's almost as if the town has been sent another message."

"That might very well be the case," Manners agreed, nodding furiously. "Yes, in fact, I'm certain of it. The sea wants us to know that it means business. This damage began at the pier, but it's crept its way throughout the town now. If Eric Grace could be taken out, that means anyone is at risk."

"You were wrong," Johnny said, turning to Harry, "Eric Grace wasn't the most important person in Crowford, but he was certainly one of the most well-known." For a moment, he once again thought back to the sight of Hazel falling down the slope. "There are more important people, and we need to protect them. No matter the cost."

"Are you coming around to our way of thinking?" Manners asked.

"I'm saying that when our town is in danger," Johnny continued, "it's our right – no, our *duty* – to step up and defend it. We're men, right? And we're honorable. No-one else knows what's really going on, not yet, but eventually they'll find out and they'll start asking why we didn't take action when we knew." He looked at Harry, then at Willy, and finally at Manners again. "So what do we have to do to sort all of this out?"

"There's only one way," Manners replied. "We have to give the sea what it wants."

"And what *does* it want?" he asked, even though he already knew the answer.

"It wants Edward Smith."

Johnny felt a shudder pass through his chest.

"Are you sure?"

Manners nodded.

"But why?" Willy said. "We still haven't figured out what he was doing on the Mercy Bell that night, or -"

"None of that matters!" Johnny snapped, turning to him. "Can't you get that through your thick head? If we sit around trying to solve every aspect of the mystery, more people are going to die and Crowford might suffer irreparable damage. We don't need to know Edward Smith's real name, not really, and we don't need to know how he ended up on that boat or what kind of nefarious things he was up to. All we need to do is deliver him to the sea, and then that's the end of it. Hopefully we can forget that he ever existed."

"I don't -"

"I said, that's the end of it!" he shouted, slamming his pint down against the table.

The others sat in silence for a moment.

"So what do we do?" Harry asked finally. "Kidnap the man?"

"He's not going to go willingly," Johnny pointed out. "I don't know about you, but I happen to love this town, and I'll do anything to keep it safe. And the people in it. If that means getting rid of one bad apple, who's caused nothing but trouble since he arrived anyway, then that's absolutely fine by me." He paused, before reaching out and putting his right hand on the center of the table. "Who's with me?"

"When are we supposing to do all of this?" Willy asked cautiously.

"If we wait, people die. So we do it tonight."

Manners reached over and put his hand on top of Johnny's.

"It's time to end this nightmare once and for all," he declared.

"I suppose I can't argue with that," Willy said, but he still hesitated before finally adding his hand to the pile. "I'm in. For the good of Crowford."

"For the good of Crowford," Harry said, and then he too added his hand.

"So it's settled," Johnny said, with a strong sense of determination in his voice. "Tonight, we're going to save Crowford. Tonight we're going to take Edward Smith and send him back where he came from. To the sea. No matter what it costs us."

CHAPTER TWENTY-TWO

KNEELING ON THE BEDROOM floor, Edward took the pack of ice and pressed it against Hazel's swollen ankle. The skin around the ankle was deeply discolored now, and after a moment Hazel let out a faint gasp of pain.

"Sorry," he said, looking up at her.

"No, it's fine," she replied. "Thank you for doing this."

"It looks pretty bad. Are you sure you shouldn't get Doctor Ford to take a look?"

"I'm certain that it'll show signs of improvement in the morning. If it doesn't, I'll drop by and see him, but honestly I just think it's a nasty sprain." She watched as he moved the pack of ice a little further up. "Have I told you that you have the most tender touch?"

"I do my best," he replied "I just can't believe what happened. I don't know what's going on, but lately it's as if this whole town's falling apart. If anything had happened to you -"

"I'm fine."

"But you could have been killed," he pointed out. "And Tobias, too. You two are the only important people in my life, and I can't stand to think that something like this happened to you. If you'd fallen differently, or if you'd landed differently, or if -"

"None of that happened," she reminded him. "Please, Edward, stop imagining the worst. We're safe, and we're here, and we're not going anywhere. Now, I have something to relieve the pain in my bag. I brought it home from the surgery a while ago. Would you mind fetching it, and then we can try to get some sleep?" She leaned down and kissed him on the forehead. "Stop worrying, darling," she continued. "We're together, and that's all that matters."

***

One hour later, standing in the doorway, Edward watched as Hazel slept. He'd tried to do the same, but eventually he'd had to get up. Now he was dressed again, and he could tell that another sleepless night was ahead. The panic about Hazel's accident had at least distracted him from the voices and the memories in his head, but now he could tell that they'd be back soon.

He looked at the cigarette in his hand, and then he turned and made his way down the stairs.

Once he was out in the back garden, he lit the cigarette and took a long drag. Up until Tobias had been born, he'd always smoked inside, but now he preferred to keep his son away from the smoke. He looked up at the starry night sky, and he listened to the sound of distant waves, and he tried to tell himself that everything was going to be alright, that the voices would eventually pass and that things would go back to normal. At the same time, he couldn't help but worry that his memories were beginning to break through, and that eventually Hazel might get hurt.

He knew he'd rather die than let anything happen to Hazel.

As he took another drag on his cigarette, he suddenly heard a faint rustling sound coming from the end of the garden. He assumed that there must be a fox nearby, but as the rustling sound continued he realized that it seemed to be caused by something larger. He knew that there was almost no chance of a burglar, since Crowford had always felt like one of the safest places in the world, but after a moment he shut the back door before making his way across the lawn, determined to find whatever was causing the noise.

Once he was down at the far end of the garden, he realized that the sound was coming from over the back wall. There was something in the alley that ran along the rear of the row of houses, and he supposed that this meant it wasn't really any of his business. Still, he took a moment to climb up onto the little pile of bricks that had been left over from an old project, and then – with the cigarette in his mouth – he leaned over the wall and looked into the alley.

In the darkness, he could barely see a thing.

"Alright, Mr. Fox?" he said after taking the cigarette out of his mouth. "We don't want any visitors tonight, thank you very much. You might as well just be on your way."

He waited, expecting to spot a fox darting to safety, but now the rustling sound had stopped.

"I don't see him!" he suddenly heard a voice shouting in his head. "Keith! Can you hear me?"

"No man could survive being down there," another voice added. "We've lost him. May the Lord have mercy on his soul, and may his family -"

"Stop it!" Edward hissed, stepping back and banging one hand against the side of his head. "Just go away! Leave me alone!"

He waited, but now the sound of the sea – which was ever-present in that part of town, so close to the shore – seemed also to be part of his memories, as if the two were bleeding together and becoming one. He put his other hand up against the side of his head and he began to squeeze, hoping that the pressure would perhaps mean that there'd be no more room for any bad thoughts. Within seconds, however, the voices had returned.

"Everyone get back to your stations! We're not giving up yet, not without a fight! I want you all to do your jobs! And as for you -"

"Stop!" Edward hissed. "Please!"

"I don't know how in God's name you ended up here, but you might as well at least be useful. Get in here and help me secure the wheel!"

"Stop!"

Dropping to his knees, Edward quickly rolled onto his side. He felt as if a huge wave of pressure was building in his mind, but that at the same time there was something stopping the wave from breaking through. His head hurt, as if it might be about to burst, and as he squeezed his eyes tight shut he began to let out a faint, pained whimper. In that moment, he truly believed that either the memories would come flooding through, or his head would split open.

Finally, however, the pressure began to ease, and he realized that he had once again failed.

Sitting up, he leaned against the wall and tried to get his breath back. He was sweating profusely, and he was so distracted by the voices he'd heard that it took a moment before he realized that three figures were standing right in front of him. Looking up, he saw that the three men were silhouetted against the night sky, but he couldn't make out any of their features.

"I..."

His voice trailed off.

"You're a right mess, aren't you?" one of the men said, stepping forward. "Alright, Mr. Smith, I think you'd better be coming with us. And please don't take that as a suggestion. Take it as more of an order."

"Who are you?" Edward stammered. "What do you want with me?"

"We're concerned citizens of Crowford," Willy said, and he too stepped forward. "This town's got a problem and it's getting bigger. We're gonna fix that problem."

"I don't know what you're talking about," Edward said, as he tried to work out how he could defend himself. "Please, I have a wife and child inside, don't hurt them."

"We're not here for them," Johnny said, and now he stepped forward just enough to let a patch of light catch one side of his face. He stared down at Edward. "We're here for you. You're coming with us, Edward Smith, whether you like it or not. Now, please, do the right thing and don't cause any fuss."

"Hurry up!" Manners hissed, from the alley.

"You're taking too long! We should be on our way by now!"

"You don't have a choice in this matter," Johnny told Edward, before reaching a hand out, offering to help him up. "You've taken a lot from Crowford, and the town's starting to pay the price. All we're here for is to make sure that you pay your dues and do the right thing. You want to do that, don't you? You want to do what's right."

Edward hesitated, before slowly taking his hand and starting to get up.

"It's the middle of the night," he pointed out cautiously. "Whatever this is about, it can wait until morning. I've got no interest in whatever foolish games you bunch of -"

Suddenly Johnny grabbed him and shoved him against the wall, before placing a hand over his mouth to keep him from crying out.

"That's just where you're wrong!" he snarled. "This is the end of the road for you, my friend! Tonight, we're going to put right something that went wrong a long time ago!"

AMY CROSS

CHAPTER TWENTY-THREE

"OKAY, NOW WHAT?" Willy asked a short while later, as they finally got Edward down to the large open green down near the shore. "Do we just shove him in?"

Struggling to get free, with a gag over his mouth to keep him quiet, Edward slammed his elbow against Willy. Before he had a chance to run, however, Johnny grabbed him by the throat and pulled him back, before putting an arm around his neck and starting to squeeze. They continued to struggle for a moment longer, but Johnny quickly gained the advantage.

"You need to accept your fate, Edward," he said firmly. "We're not even doing anything to you, not really. We're just putting right our mistake."

Edward tried to reply, but he wasn't able to

get any words out. He hadn't stopped struggling since he'd been dragged away from his home, and his eyes darted about as he tried to figure out exactly how he was going to escape. His mind was racing, too, and he felt certain that he'd get another opportunity. And this time, he'd find a way to make it count.

"We need to take him down to the water's edge," Manners said, watching the darkness carefully in case the three ghosts appeared. "I don't know exactly what will happen then, but I'm quite certain that they'll take him." He looked toward the large, dark lighthouse station, but there was still no sign of movement. "They must know that we're close. They've been waiting five years for this night. Come on, we have to make things right. And if we do, they might give up some of their secrets."

"Give up their secrets?" Willy asked. "What do you mean?"

"Move!" Johnny said, shoving Edward forward with such force that he sent him thudding down onto his knees. "Get up!"

He hauled Edward up and shoved him again, and this time the man stumbled but managed to stay on his feet. His eyes were filled with fear, but he was quickly shoved forward again as the others forced him to make his way across the grass. Every few seconds he tried to turn and run, but he was being pushed from all sides and finally they reached the path that separated the grass from the beach. Little wooden huts dotted the landscape leading down to the shore, along with several boats and assorted fishing equipment.

"Man, it's cold out here," Willy said, starting to shiver. "Even for January, this is freezing!"

"They have to be here somewhere," Manners muttered, walking ahead of the others, his footsteps crunching on the shingle. "We just have to be patient. After all this time, they won't wait long to take him. And when they come, they'll be grateful."

As they reached the shoreline at the bottom of the sloping beach, they all looked out at the darkness.

Suddenly Edward turned and punched Willy, knocking him down, before slipping free of Harry and racing back up the beach. Muttering a few choice expletives under his breath, Johnny immediately set off after him, and he quickly managed to grab him and drag him down. Landing on top of the fleeing man, Johnny struggled for a moment to get him under control, and in the process Edward finally managed to slip free of the gag.

"Is this about Hazel?" he snapped.

"What do you mean?" Johnny asked.

"I know about you and her," he continued. "I've seen the way you look at her. Ever since I arrived here, you've been moping after her like a lovesick puppy!"

"You don't know what you're talking about," Johnny sneered.

"I'm right, though, aren't I? You think that if you can get rid of me, she'll be yours."

"You're not -"

"She'll never love a murderer!" Edward hissed. "You know that, right? You can kill me, but it won't change anything between you and Hazel. You can even try to fool yourself, you can tell yourself over and over again that you're doing this for the good of the town, but we both know that you're lying. And the truth will eat you up on the inside, until there's nothing left of you but a hollow shell!"

"I don't have to listen to this," Johnny said, although there was a hint of uncertainty in his voice. "You don't know anything about me."

Edward spat at him, hitting him in the eye.

"Goddammit!" Johnny snarled, wiping the saliva away before stepping back and hauling Edward up onto his feet. "This is about Crowford! This is about saving the town from all the pain and fear that *you* brought here. We should have left you to drown out there five years ago. I don't know who you are or what you did or where you came from, but you've brought nothing but misery to Crowford. That ends tonight. You're going back out there to face whatever justice the sea has in store for you."

"Whatever justice the sea has in store for me?" Edward replied with a smirk. "Listen to yourself, man. You're insane. You've let this lovelorn puppy shtick turn you into a pathetic moron!"

"You need to learn when to shut up," Johnny replied. "We're not -"

Before he could finish, Edward lunged at him. Johnny tried to step out of the way, but Edward managed to turn and hit him in the chest, sending him falling backward. As Edward once again tried to run, Johnny stumbled up and reached out, grabbing his leg and hauling him down. Harry and Willy raced over to help, but they stood back and watched as Johnny spun Edward around and then punched him hard in the face, knocking out several teeth and sending blood bursting from the man's lip.

"That's how we deal with unwanted people around here," Johnny said breathlessly, getting to his feet and then hauling Edward up by the collar. "It's over for you, do you hear me?"

"Go to -"

Johnny punched him again, even harder this time, almost knocking him out. Still holding onto him by the collar, he waited until Edward looked up at him again. The man's face was bloodied and cut, and he looked to be on the verge of losing consciousness.

"No-one else is ever going to suffer in

Crowford because of you," Johnny continued. "Not one man or woman or child. We came here tonight to keep our town safe, and that's exactly what we're going to do. Fortunately, it doesn't really matter whether or not you agree to that, or whether you understand. It's going to happen anyway."

He hesitated, and then – filled with one final burst of rage – he punched Edward again.

"Johnny, no!" Hazel screamed.

Turning, Johnny saw to his shock that Hazel was scrambling down the beach, limping heavily as she raced toward them. Frozen in place, not quite able to work out what was happening, Johnny tried to think of something to say, of some way to explain himself. He couldn't get any words out, however, not even as Hazel pulled Edward away from him and began to examine his bloodied face.

"What are you doing?" she shouted at them. "Are you all insane?"

"It's not what it looks like," Johnny stammered, before glancing down and seeing the blood on his own knuckles.

"Edward, can you hear me?" Hazel sobbed, as her husband let out a faint murmur. "Edward, it's me, I'm here. I knew something was wrong as soon as I realized you were missing. I don't know how, I just had this feeling that something awful was happening."

"You need to listen to me," Johnny said,

stepping toward her. "Hazel -"

"Get away from us, you bastard!" she shouted, with tears in her eyes. "Don't come near me!"

"I'm sorry," Johnny stammered, as he watched her cradling Edward in her arms. "You have to believe me, I never wanted it to be like this."

"They're here," Manners said suddenly.

Johnny froze, and in that moment he realized that the air all around felt so much colder than before. At the same time, he was able to hear a splashing sound coming from the water. For a few seconds, he was too scared to look, but then he saw that Hazel's expression was filled with horror as she stared past him. Slowly, he turned and saw three ghostly figures emerging from the water and stepping up onto the beach, and he realized that he recognized all three men.

Percy Weaver.

Keith Simmons.

And Captain John Lund.

All three of them had died five years earlier, when the *Mercy Belle* had gone down, and all three were now back. Their faces were pale and gaunt, and worms and other creatures from the sea squirmed and wriggled in gaps in their flesh. A terrible rotten stench filled the air, and Johnny swallowed hard as he realized without a shadow of a doubt that he was staring at three dead men.

"I'm out of here!" Willy gasped, and he and Harry turned and scrambled away up the beach.

"The time has come," Captain Lund said, his voice sounding gravelly and damaged as he took a step forward. "We have come for him. Now we shall take him."

CHAPTER TWENTY-FOUR

"THIS ISN'T REAL," Hazel said, her voice filled with fear as – still cradling her husband – she stared at the ghosts. "This... None of this can be real."

As he watched Captain Lund and the other two men stepping closer, Johnny was seized by a sense of abject terror. Part of him wanted to turn and run like Willy and Harry, to just get away from the beach and pretend that he had nothing to do with the unfolding horror, but somehow he managed to stay rooted to the spot. No matter how scared he might have been, he knew he couldn't leave without Hazel.

"I have brought him to you!" Manners said, holding his hands out and stepping in front of Captain Lund. "See? I did what Father Warden could not, and I delivered the one you have wanted for so long. I was hoping that might mean you could see your way to... cutting a deal with me. Hear me out, I only want to know about the mysteries of the sea. Couldn't you see your way to helping me with that?"

"Is this really happening?" Hazel whimpered. "Please, tell me it's not happening..."

Johnny turned to her and saw that Edward, though bloodied and bruised, was starting to sit up.

"Tell me!" Hazel shouted. "Johnny, what's going on here?"

"It's a little bit complicated," he replied, fully aware that this was something of an understatement. "I think the best way to describe it is -"

Before he could get another word out, he heard Manners let out a scream, and he turned just in time to see that the old man was down on his knees. Captain Lund had reached a hand into Manners' chest and was holding him tight, and a moment later Manners began to vomit cold, slimy, dirty seawater.

"We will strike no bargains," Captain Lund intoned darkly, staring down at Manners with an expression that was utterly devoid of compassion. "You should have been satisfied with your role, which was to offer up the one we seek. For your greed, and your belief that you could ever possibly understand the mysteries that exist out there beyond the shore, you must now pay a heavy price. The mysteries of the sea are not for any man to comprehend."

"No!" Manners gurgled, as seawater began to flow from his eyes, pushing the balls out of their sockets. "I'm sorry! I take it back! I -"

In an instant, he let out a loud groan as blood began to gush from his mouth, mixed with more seawater. At the same time, his throat began to split open, allowing the immense pressure of even more water to burst through. His body started shuddering, and now even his fingers were breaking open as he began to fill with a vast amount of seawater. Like a sack of skin getting filled well past its breaking point, he started to swell like a balloon, until his body broke apart in several spots and he slumped down dead against the pebbles.

Staring in horror at what was left of the old man, Johnny didn't at first notice the sound of footsteps over his shoulder, stumbling up the beach. Finally turning, he saw that Hazel was helping Edward to get away, and a moment later the pair of them disappeared over the crest.

"Now," Captain Lund said, "we shall have the one we seek."

Filled with panic, Johnny got to his feet and hurried after Hazel and Edward. He stumbled a couple of times, almost slipping all the way back down the slope, but finally he made it all the way up to the line of fishing boats at the top, at which point he turned and saw that the three dead men were slowly making their way after him. He tried to think of something he might be able to do or say to persuade them to stop, but they looked hellish in the moonlight and he quickly realized that he'd only end up suffering the same fate as Manners.

Turning, he hurried between the boats and finally reached the path. He stopped for a moment and looked around, and after a couple of seconds he spotted Hazel and Edward in the distance. They were making for the large, open doorway of the lifeboat station.

"No!" Johnny hissed, realizing that they were making a huge mistake. "Don't go in there!"

Almost immediately, Hazel helped Edward into the station and they disappeared from view. Johnny looked back down the beach and saw the dead men still following, and then he set out across the grass.

"Hey, guys!" he called out as he got closer to the lighthouse station. "Hazel! You can't hide in there, it won't work! We need to go somewhere else and get help, okay?"

As he reached the station and looked through the enormous open doorway, he saw the *James Furnham* resting in the darkness. It had been many years seen he'd last seen that boat, since in the aftermath of the *Mercy Belle* disaster he'd slowly drifted away from volunteer work on the lifeboat, and for a moment he was struck by the sight of the large, proud boat still waiting for the next time it was called into action.

Looking over his shoulder he saw that Captain Lund and the other two men had reached the top of the beach and were continuing their relentless, albeit slow, pursuit.

"This isn't going to work," he muttered, before stepping through into the icy air of the lifeboat station. "Hazel!" he called out. "We have to go!"

"Help us!" she shouted.

Realizing that time was running out, Johnny turned and began to close the huge wooden doors. Although the job usually required three men, he was just about able to get the two doors to swing shut, and then he slid the bolt across. He had no real belief that the door would keep Captain Lund and the others out for long, but as he took a couple of steps backward he figured that at least it might buy them some time.

Turning, he made his way around the side of the lifeboat, and then he heard a thudding sound coming from somewhere high up. He reached the ladder and began to climb up, and finally he saw that Hazel was tending gently to Edward on the deck. Caught in a patch of moonlight that was shining through a hole in the roof, Hazel was trying to clean one of the wounds on Edward's face, and after a moment she turned to Johnny.

"Where are they?" she asked.

"We can't hide here," he replied. "They know where we are."

"He couldn't go any further."

"That doesn't mean -"

"You damn near beat him to a pulp, Johnny!"

"No, I..."

His voice trailed off for a few seconds, but deep down he knew she was right.

"What do you need?" he asked finally. "This isn't the time for talking, it's the time for getting out of here. What do you need, to make it so he can walk?"

"Water," she replied.

"I can get that."

"And a towel."

"That too."

"And it's so cold in here. Do you have a blanket, something like that?"

"I think so." He hesitated, seeing Edward's bloodied face and realizing that he was responsible for the man's latest injuries. He quickly turned and climbed back down the ladder. "I'll gather what I can, but we have to hurry. I don't know how much time we have, or what they'll do when they get here, but we don't have long. We need to find someone who can help us!"

As soon as he got to the bottom of the ladder, he made his way around to the other end of the station, where a small break room contained a few essential supplies. He was trying hard not to panic, although he couldn't help but think back to the sight of Manners' body getting split open. He also felt furious that Willy and Harry had deserted them as soon as the ghosts had arrived, but at the same time he understood their fear.

Stopping in the break room, he was about to head to the barrels in the corner when he spotted the small back door. He froze, and in an instant he realized that he had another option. He could still stick to the original plan and find a way to turn Edward Smith over to the ghosts, and that way he'd be able to save the entire town. Sure, Hazel would be furious, but he figured she'd have to understand eventually. All the pain and fear could be over relatively quickly, if he only could find the courage to follow through on everything he'd agreed with Manners.

A moment later, realizing that he couldn't betray Hazel, he stepped over to the door and drew the bolt across.

AMY CROSS

CHAPTER TWENTY-FIVE

"HOW'S IT GOING BACK here?" Hazel asked a couple of minutes later, as she limped through. "Do you have any medical equipment? I was thinking there might be something I can use."

"There's a box here," Johnny replied, opening a drawer and pulling out one of the kits that they used to take out on the boat during an emergency. "Maybe it's got something you need."

He was still filling a bucket with water. Glancing over at her, he saw that she was sorting through the kit. He waited for her to say something, and after a few seconds he realized that she seemed to be intentionally ignoring him.

"It wasn't how it looked back there," he said finally. "You have to believe me."

"So you weren't beating my husband to a pulp as you prepared to deliver him to a bunch of ghosts?" She looked at him. "I overheard enough down there to put the pieces together, Johnny. Please don't insult me by acting as if I got it all wrong."

"They want him really bad," he replied. "Whatever he did before we rescued him, whatever happened out there on the *Mercy Belle* -"

"Whatever happened out there doesn't matter anymore!" she snapped angrily. "Can't you get that through your thick head? It's in the past!"

"Not to those ghosts," he pointed out. "Not to the sea."

"The sea is just water!"

"No, it's something else as well," he replied. "I don't understand it, I don't think anyone does, but Manners said that Crowford has a kind of agreement or compact with the sea, and I think there might be something to that idea. Lund and the other ghosts have gone to a great deal of trouble to get Edward back, Hazel, and who are we to say that they don't have that right?"

She froze, staring at him.

"What if Edward did something really bad?" he continued. "They wouldn't be coming after him without a reason."

"I can't believe you said that," she replied icily, before turning her attention back to the medical kit. Her hands were trembling as she sorted through its contents. "There's nothing useful in here. It's hopeless!"

"I'm not a bad person," he told her.

"Are you sure about that?"

"All my life I've felt like I'm walking a really narrow line between being good and bad," he continued. "I never knew which side I'd ultimately end up on, but I'm not ready to make that choice tonight."

"You think it's a choice?" she asked.

"I think we're caught up in something we can't possibly understand," he said cautiously. "You've seen what's been happening to the town. It's falling apart, and people – good people – are dying. Do you really think that the life of one man, whoever he is, is worth all that?"

"You really mean it, don't you?" she replied, with tears in her eyes. "You want to just let them take him."

"What if he did something *really* bad?" Johnny asked. "It'd have to be pretty awful to justify them still coming for him, right? Okay, sure, maybe he's a good husband and a good father now, but what if he did something terrible in the past? And what if nothing can make up for that? What if there's just a kind of natural order to the world, and we have no right to stand in its way?"

He waited for her to reply, but he was starting to realize that he'd never be able to persuade her. Hazel Christie had always been able to see the best in people; that was one of the reasons he'd fallen for her all those years ago, and he supposed it was also one of the reasons why she'd stuck by him whenever he'd caused trouble as a boy. The thing he loved most about her was also the thing that perhaps meant they could now never be together.

"I'm only saying it how it is," he added finally.

"You didn't go to war, Johnny, did you?"

"What's that got to do with anything?"

"You were right at the tail-end. You were put into training, along with your pals, but you never actually ended up fighting."

"I don't see what -"

"I just wonder how you'd have done out there," she continued, "if your attitude is basically to surrender whenever things seem bleak."

"That's not fair!"

"Isn't it?" She stared at him for a moment. "I'm sure they taught you a lot during your training, but that's no substitute for actually being out there on the battlefield. I hate war, Johnny. I saw things, as a nurse, that will stay with me forever. I saw men with the most horrific injuries, I sat with them and held their hands as they died, and I saw how the survivors were changed by what they went through."

"So is that why you married Edward Smith?" he asked. "Did you see him as just another injured soldier?"

"I married him because -"

She stopped herself before she could finish that sentence.

"You can't have loved him," Johnny said, "not really. Not so quickly."

"I -"

"I don't buy that for one second," he continued. "The way I see it, you got so used to feeling sorry for people with war injuries, you couldn't stop yourself falling for the guy even though he only *looked* like he -"

Before he could say another word, Hazel slapped him hard, hard enough to shock him and make him take a step back.

"Don't you ever say anything like that ever again!" she hissed. "You're just a boy, Johnny! You're old enough to be a man, but you're no better than a child!" She hesitated, and then she closed the medical kit. "We don't have time for this," she added, turning and limping to the door. "I have to get Edward into a fit state so he can walk, and then I have to get him away from those wretched things!"

"I'm sorry," Johnny said.

She turned to him, and she still had tears in her eyes.

"I don't care," she told him. "You're no more than a deadbeat bum, anyway. You don't even have a job. You and your pals just float around, picking up money here and there, then drinking it all. That's not the way to live a meaningful life, Johnny. That's the way to end up sad and alone. If you live your life this way, who's going to care about you? Who's going to be there for you? Who's going to tend your grave when you're gone?" She paused. "Maybe I was wrong about you all this time. And maybe I was wrong about -"

Suddenly she froze, as they both heard a distant rumbling sound coming from the main part of the building. They both listened for a moment, but it was Johnny who realized first what they were hearing.

"The doors," he whispered, before hurrying past Hazel and back out toward the hall where the lifeboat was kept. "I don't know how, but they must have found a way to open the -"

And then he saw the truth.

At the far end of the main hall, a solitary figure was struggling as he slowly but surely managed to push the huge wooden doors open. The figure slipped slightly, almost falling, but he managed to keep upright and finally he got the doors to part, and then he stood in the opening. Outside, in the cold night, the ghosts of Captain Lund and his two men stood waiting, and finally Edward – who had somehow summoned the energy to stand – took a couple of faltering steps toward them.

"No!" Hazel screamed, rushing after him, only for Johnny to hold her back. "Edward, what are you doing?"

Slowly, Edward turned and looked back at her.

"Let go of me!" she shouted at Johnny, but he was gripping her firmly. She looked at Edward again. "Edward, get back in here!"

"I can't let anyone else suffer because of me," Edward told her, his voice faltering slightly. "I can't let *you* suffer, Hazel, or Tobias."

"Don't go with them!" she screamed.

"This is how it has to be," he continued, "and by dragging it out, I'm only putting more people at risk." He paused for a moment. "The past five years have made me so happy, but I've come to love this town and I refuse to be the reason for its suffering. And you, Hazel... what I feel for you is far more than love, it's something that has made my life worth living. Whatever happens to me next, I promise that I'll be thinking of you until the end. I will always love you."

"No," Hazel sobbed, as tears streamed down her face. "Please..."

Edward looked at her for a moment longer, and then he turned and took a slow, unsteady step out toward the three ghostly figures. Holding his arms out, he looked into their dead eyes and prepared for the end.

"I'm here," he told them, as they slowly began to move toward him. "Spare this town and everyone in it, and take me!"

"Edward," Hazel cried, "don't do this..."

"Just promise me that Crowford will be left alone now," Edward continued, as his voice trembled with fear. "That's all I ask. Promise me that no-one else has to suffer because of whatever I did."

Captain Lund stopped in front of him.

"No!" Johnny shouted suddenly, grabbing one of the flare guns from a wall rack and racing toward the opening. "Stop!"

With that, he fired the flare gun past Edward, hitting the ground directly in front of Captain Lund and the others ghosts, causing a vast wall of red light and heat to explode through the night air.

CHAPTER TWENTY-SIX

"WHAT ARE YOU DOING?" Edward snapped, as Johnny tried to pull him back. "Let go of me!"

"I'm afraid I can't do that," Johnny told him. "There has to be another way."

"Are you insane?" Edward said, struggling to get free as the flare burned close to them. "It's too late, I have to go with them!"

"If you do, it'll break Hazel's heart," Johnny replied, and he managed to pull him back a few steps. "I don't know what we're going to do, I don't know how we're going to stop all of this, but we're not going to surrender, okay? We're *never* going to surrender. We're going to get you away from here and then we're going to find someone who can help us."

"You can't argue with these things! You're

not going to be able to make them change their minds! They're not going to stop coming for me until they get what they want!"

Before Johnny could reply, they both turned and saw that Captain Lund and the other two ghosts were stepping directly through the wall of red light that was still burning on the ground.

"We will take the one we came for now," Captain Lund said firmly, before reaching forward with a bony, rotten hand and grabbing hold of Johnny's shoulder. "You," he snarled. "We have waited a long time for you."

"Me?" Johnny replied, too shocked for a moment to know how he should react. "I don't mean to be rude, but I think you might be a little confused."

"*I'm* the one you want," Edward stammered. "It's always been me!"

"Exactly," Johnny added. "Please don't take this the wrong way, but I think there's been a bit of a mistake."

"You have always been the one we want," Captain Lund said, tightening his grip on Johnny as the other two ghosts stepped around him. "Now you will come to us, back to where you belong, and you will pay for what you did!"

"No," Edward said, trying to push him away, "you've got this all back to front, it was -"

Suddenly one of the other ghosts grabbed

him from behind and pulled him back, before shoving him to the ground. For a bunch of dead men, they certainly had some power, and Johnny was already starting to realize that he couldn't simply fight his way out of trouble. Still, he knew that he had to get through to them somehow, because they seemed to have made a terrible mix-up. There was no way that *he* could have been their target all along.

"We have waited five years to get you," Captain Lund told him. "We shall wait no longer."

"Yeah, about that," Johnny said, struggling to get the words out, "you guys are really messing this whole thing up. I'm not the guy you're after, I'm the guy who's trying to *save* the guy you're after and -"

Before he could say another word, the captain grabbed the back of his neck and dug his fingers' bony tips deep into the flesh. Crying out, Johnny dropped to his knees as he felt blood running down his back, but in an instant he was twisted around and he found himself powerless to resist as Captain Lund began to drag him down to the beach. Reaching up, he tried to somehow push the dead man's hands away, but he could already feel an icy paralysis spreading throughout his body as his feet began to trail across the shingle.

"Stop!" he heard Edward shouting, already sounding so far away now. "It's not him you want!

It's me!"

"You've made a mistake," Johnny gasped, as he began to feel much weaker. "You've got the wrong... man..."

No matter how hard he struggled, however, he was unable to break free, and he could already feel the sloping beach getting steeper beneath him as he was taken closer to the shoreline. He managed to twist around just enough to look out at the water, and to his horror he saw that a small wooden boat was waiting for them all. Filled with a profound sense of terror that immediately burst through his body, he tried yet again to escape Captain Lund's icy grip, but deep down he could tell that there was no way to get free.

"You've got the wrong man," he said again, struggling to raise his voice so that it might be heard. "Don't you see that? It's Edward you want, not me!"

"We do not make mistakes," Captain Lund replied darkly, as he dragged Johnny out into the shallow water at the shore. "We have never had any interest in that other man. But when you rescued him, you reminded the sea of your crime, and we were sent to track you down. The town had five years to deliver you. Now you belong to us."

"That doesn't even make any sense!" Johnny gasped, looking back toward the shore and seeing the last of the flare's glow starting to die down.

"Please, just stop and think about this for one moment and you'll realize that you've got the wrong man!"

As those words left his lips, he saw a figure running into view at the top of the beach. The figure began to hurry down toward the shore, and Johnny realized that it must be Edward.

Suddenly he was hauled up and thrown over the side of the boat, and sent crashing down against the damp wooden boards. He tried to scramble to his feet, but Captain Lund shoved him toward the other end and let out an angry, warning snarl.

"This can't be happening," Johnny stammered, crawling to the other end of the boat and then turning to see that the three dead men were climbing in after him. "It's a dream. It's all just a dream and I'm going to wake up at any moment."

Just as Captain Lund joined the others on the boat, Edward fired the flare gun, but the flare merely hit the water next to the boat and sizzled to nothing. Edward fired again, and again he missed, this time firing too long. The second flare seared through the sky, forcing Johnny to duck down, but then it harmlessly hit the water. Johnny knew that there would only be one more flare in the gun, but a moment later Edward fired again, this time hitting the water on the other side of the boat.

"Bring him back here!" Johnny heard Edward shouting. "It's me you want!"

The boat tilted dramatically as Captain Lund took his position, and then again as the other two dead sailors began to row. Johnny grabbed the boat's sides, ready to leap out and try to swim for the shore, but then he froze as he saw Captain Lund's stern gaze. In that moment, he realized that even if he tried to jump out and get back onto dry land, he'd simply be caught and returned to the boat. Still, he had to try.

Reaching up, he touched the back of his neck and felt the deep cuts that marked the spot where Captain Lund had taken hold of him. More blood was running from the wounds, and he could still feel a chill in his bones, but he knew that he only had one final shot at getting away.

He sat up a little, and then – in a flash – he made his move.

Throwing himself over the side of the boat, he crashed into the water, only for one of the oars to smack straight into his head. He managed to dive down deeper until he hit the shingles on the seabed, and then he tried to haul himself back toward the shore. Before he made it more than half a meter, however, he felt an icy hand once again grabbing him by the scruff of the neck, and he screamed as he was pulled out of the water. Twisting around, he found himself face to face with Captain Lund.

"You will not escape your fate," the captain growled. "You must pay for your crime."

In that moment, Johnny was struck by the most intensely foul stink of dead, rotten flesh. He could see through the holes in the captain's face, and he spotted small creatures that seemed to have made their home in the midst of all that tattered meat. The man's eyeballs, meanwhile, were split down the middle and their blackened insides were glistening in the moonlight.

"Johnny!" Hazel screamed from the shore. "Come back!"

Before he had a chance to react, Johnny was spun around and slammed back down into the boat, so hard this time that his head hit one of the wooden boards and he was knocked out instantly. The very last thing he was aware of, before losing consciousness, was the tilt of the boat, along with the faint and distant sound of Hazel still shouting his name on the shore.

CHAPTER TWENTY-SEVEN

AS SOON AS HE began to stir, Johnny realized that he could feel a boat beneath him, bobbing about on the waves. He opened his eyes and saw darkness, but after a moment he remembered everything that had happened that night. He hesitated, hoping against hope that perhaps there had been some mistake, that he might have imagined the whole thing, but then he slowly turned and looked toward the other end of the boat, and he saw Captain Lund and the two other dead men staring back at him.

They'd stopped rowing.

"Ah, hell," Johnny whispered to himself, feeling a throbbing pain on the side of his head as he carefully, and painfully, began to sit up.

Looking all around, he saw that they were far out from the shore. The lights of Crowford were just about visible, several miles to the west, but Johnny knew he'd never be able to swim that far. Turning the other way, he realized that the little wooden boat had come to a stop surrounded by several of the smaller sandbanks.

"Should they be doing that?" he asked, furrowing his brow as he realized that the sandbanks would ordinarily only appear at low tide. "Never mind," he continued, turning to look at the dead men again, "I'm sure there's some explanation that I wouldn't understand anyway."

He sat up a little more, and the boat continued to bob beneath him.

"So," he said after a moment, "Captain Lund, huh? Long time, no see. And Percy, Keith, you look..."

He stared at their skeletal faces.

"We tried to save you," he continued, struggling to keep from panicking. "You have to believe me, we were out there in that storm and we did everything in our power to get to you. The storm was just too strong, and by the time we got there the *Mercy Belle* had been destroyed." He looked at Percy, and then at Keith. "We looked for your bodies, but they were gone. No-one could have done anything more for you."

He waited, but none of the men replied.

"I don't know how much clearer I need to make this," he said finally, "but I think I'm not the guy you were originally looking for. I'm -"

"We know who you are," Captain Lund said, and now his skull creaked slightly as he spoke. "You are the one who trespassed all those years ago. Worse, you are the one who stole. Trespassing is tolerated. Theft is not."

"I beg your pardon?" Johnny asked, as he started shivering in the cold night air. "I've never stolen anything in my life. Wait, you're not talking about the shrimp, are you?"

"The shrimp do not belong to the sand."

"Then what are you talking about?" Johnny snapped. "I never took a goddamn thing!"

"You stole treasure from the deep," the captain continued. "All treasure that falls into the sandbanks must *stay* in the sandbanks."

"I really don't know what you're talking about," Johnny said. "I've not even been to the sandbanks a lot, mostly it was just when I was a kid and -"

Stopping suddenly, he remembered that day – many years earlier – when he'd been out there with his uncle, and with Hazel. He'd found a little metal sphere that day, just a piece of junk from some shipwreck, but it had been covered in cuts and dents and for some reason he'd found it interesting. He'd dug it out of the sand and tried to take it home, primarily because he'd hoped – yet again – to impress Hazel. Then his uncle had spotted it and pulled it out of his hands and thrown it back into the sea. He remembered how annoyed he'd been at the time, but since that day – twenty years earlier – he'd maybe thought of that little sphere a grand total of half a dozen times.

"You've got to be kidding me," he whispered, before looking at Captain Lund again. "You have *got* to be yanking my chain!"

"Nobody steals from the sands," the captain replied.

"It was twenty years ago!" he shouted. "I didn't even take it home! My uncle threw it back!"

"Into the sea, perhaps," Captain Lund said, "but not back into the sands. You broke the covenant that day, and the sand remembers. It might never have come after you, though, if you hadn't attracted its attention again five years ago. When you jumped into the water to save that man, the sand was angered. It was as if you were celebrating your disobedience. You returned recently, but the sands almost took the wrong man. After that, they had to rest. Now, once again, they are ready for you."

"You're nuts," Johnny stammered. "Sand doesn't have a mind. And even if it did, I did *nothing* to get on its bad side! It was Edward you wanted, the guy we pulled out of the water. He's the guy who caused the *Mercy Belle* to get smashed to pieces."

"The Mercy Belle was destroyed by a storm," Captain Lund replied, "like so many boats before it. Like so many boats out here, that were struck down either by the elements or by the sand itself."

"So it was never about Edward?" Johnny asked, as he began to understand the truth. "That was a misunderstanding, huh? I suppose we all assumed it was him, seeing as how no-one really liked him to begin with. But all that time... it was *me* you were after. And all because of some stupid trinket that I don't even have anymore."

"It is not your place to bargain for your soul," Captain Lund told him. "The sands punish as they see fit. We are merely its servants. The sand is our master."

Johnny opened his mouth to reply, but at that moment he realized he could see another vessel nearby. Hoping for a moment that he might now be saved, he got to his feet and raised his arms to wave, but then he saw that the vessel was some kind of old-time sailing ship, and that it appeared to be frozen in place. Looking around, he saw more boats, hundreds and hundreds of them, ranging in size from tiny rowboats to huge old galleons. He knew there was no way that so many boats could all be out at one time off the coast of Crowford, and as an icy wind blew against him he realized that he wasn't necessarily seeing the present day.

He was seeing the past.

He was seeing the ghosts of all the men who had died in the cold, dark waters just a few miles from Crowford's shore. Each face that stared back at him was the face of a man who had died, probably in terror, certainly far from home, and whose body no doubt lay in the depths. For a moment, Johnny was unable to stop looking at so many dead souls. At the same time, he was starting to realize that he could hear a faint whisper coming from some of them, floating in the cold air all around.

"Join us," they seemed to be saying, and more and more of them were adding their voices to the chorus. "Join us."

"The sands never forget those who die here," Captain Lund explained, getting to his feet and walking up behind Johnny. "Not their names, not their faces, and not their vessels."

Barely hearing a word that the dead man had said, Johnny was instead looking at the figures up on the deck of one of the larger boats. They all had a ghostly appearance, and as he looked at some of the other vessels he realized that they too were manned by the faint whispers of long-dead men. Some were dressed in fairly modern clothing, while others looked to have come from centuries long past. Surrounded by the dead, Johnny finally came to understand that the mysteries of the sea were beyond anything he could possibly comprehend.

"It was always you we were after," Captain Lund said, standing right behind him now. "The sands sent us. It was not the revenge of the *Mercy Belle* that Crowford should have been fearing. It was the revenge of the sands. Now we are delivering you for justice, and that means we – the crew of the noblest fishing boat that ever sailed these seas – will finally be allowed to rest in our eternal slumber."

"But..."

Johnny's voice trailed off, and then he turned to the dead man.

"The sands are our master," Captain Lund sneered.

"Sure, but they also seem kinda petty," Johnny pointed out. "Honestly, all I did was take a lousy -"

Suddenly Captain Lund pushed him hard, sending him hurtling over the side of the little boat and crashing down into the sea. He landed on a barely submerged patch of sand, but instantly he felt himself being drawn deeper beneath the surface, and he found that the more he struggled, the more the sand seemed to grip hold of him and pull him into its realm. He gasped for air, trying to fill his lungs, but in that moment his head dipped into the water and he felt the suction of the sand as it turned him around and consumed him completely. As he sank deeper and deeper into the darkness, he couldn't even scream.

CHAPTER TWENTY-EIGHT

ENCASED IN COLD, WET sand, Johnny was unable to move. His mouth was wide open, locked in that final attempt at a scream, and clumps of sand had already begun to crumble down to the back of his throat. His hands were reaching out to the sides, and with the fingers of his left hand he could just about feel something hard and shiny. A skull, he assumed. He no longer knew which way was up and which way was down, and his eyes – which remained open, even as grains of sand pressed against them – saw only darkness.

How long had it been since his last breath?

Two minutes at least, maybe more.

All he could think about was Hazel, and the fact that there was so much he'd never said to her. He tried to comfort himself with the thought that she probably knew anyway, that she understood how he felt, but he hated the fact that he'd never been brave enough to actually say the words. Now the chance was gone, and in truth it had disappeared on the night when Edward Smith had first arrived in Crowford. All he could do now was hope that Hazel would be happy, and that she wouldn't mourn him too much, and that she'd go on with her life as a wife and mother. In fact, he hoped that she'd forget him, save perhaps for a few moments here and there. No, not even moments. He wanted her to be blissfully happy. For the first time in his life, right at the brink of death, he didn't one about himself at all. Only her. He wanted her to forget he'd ever existed, to not even bother going to his grave.

Two and a half minutes had passed now, almost three.

His lungs were screaming, but he couldn't move an inch. Too much sand was packed in tight all around him, pressing him down. After a moment, however, he felt himself shift slightly, as a current in the sand turned him to one side and then pushed him along. He realized he must be going deeper and deeper into the darkness, and that eventually he'd reach the spot that would become his final resting spot. More sand fell into his mouth and crumbled down to the back of his throat, driven in by the force of his body getting pulled along. His mouth was almost full now, and his nostrils too, and the sand was pressing against his eyes with such firmness that he felt as if the eyeballs might burst inward.

And then, suddenly, he realized that the tip of his right index finger was poking out of the sand. He could feel cold wind and rain blowing against his skin, and a moment later the whole world seemed to rumble around him.

***

Gasping for air, with pain screaming through every inch of his body, Johnny finally hauled himself up through the sand and felt the wind against his face. He began to gag, vomiting up huge quantities of sand and feeling the sharp little grains cutting against the back of his throat. Leaning forward, he shook his head, dislodging some of the sand that had been packed around his face, and he tried furiously to blink away the sand that had not only scratched his eyes but that had also slipped behind his eyelids.

Thunder rumbled in the sky above, and a moment later a flash of lightning lit the sandbank as Johnny scrambled fully out of the hole and rolled onto his side. He splashed down into a shallow pool of water, startling a solitary shrimp that quickly scurried away, and then he rolled onto his back and looked up at the stormy sky that sent rain crashing down all around. Another flash of lightning arced across the sky, and a moment later another rumble of thunder seemed to cause the entire sandbank to shudder slightly.

Still coughing up sand, Johnny stared to sit up. He was in so much pain, he could barely even think, and he was still struggling to blink all the sand out of his eyes. At least he could see now, however, and – as he looked around – another flash of lightning briefly lit up the bare, empty sandbank. He had no idea how he'd managed to escape from the cold, sandy tomb beneath the surface, but he was sure that he'd not really had anything to do with the process. It was as if the sandbank itself had changed its mind and had decided to spit him out.

Out into the middle of nowhere.

Somehow, through the pain, Johnny managed to stand. His feet splashed in the pool of water as he steadied himself. He began to look around, but in all the wind and rain he couldn't really see anything, save for when a flash of lightning briefly illuminated the scene. It took a moment for him to realize that there was no longer any sign of all the ghostly vessels he'd seen earlier, or of Captain Lund and his men, and then he remembered that there had been no storm at all when he'd left Crowford. The bad weather must have come on very suddenly.

Shivering in the rain, he tried to hug himself

for warmth, but he succeeded only in pressing his cold, drenched clothes tighter against his body. He was relieved to be out of the sand, but at the same time he knew there was no way to get back to Crowford. As another bolt of lightning sparked across the sky, Johnny found himself looking out at the sea and wondering whether he'd have any chance of swimming all the way home. At first, he assumed that any attempt would be suicide, but then he realized that it might be better than freezing to death on the sandbank. In his current state, he knew he wouldn't last until morning, and that even then he was unlikely to be found. He began to stumble across the sand, making for the water's edge, and he tried to encourage himself by focusing on the positives.

At least if he tried to swim, he'd have a chance.

A tiny, infinitesimally small chance... but a chance.

Stopping for a moment, he tried to summon the courage and strength to start. After all, why would the sand have changed its mind and saved him, only to condemn him to a cold and lonely death? He made the sign of the cross against his chest; he'd never been particularly religious, but he'd been forced to go to church every Sunday as a child and he supposed there was no harm in trying, and then he began to wade down the slope of the sandbank, splashing into the sea and immediately feeling the waves crashing against him. His optimism began to slip, and he felt that he was facing certain death, but he reminded himself once more that he had to at least try. Nancy was out there somewhere, waiting, and -

No.

He stopped himself just in time.

Nancy was Edward's wife, and that wasn't ever going to change. He knew that there was no point still pining for her, and that he couldn't even use her for motivation. He had to accept that any chance he had with Nancy was now over. He was alone.

That didn't mean, however, that he couldn't at least *try* to swim.

And then, out in the darkness, he saw a flash of light.

He froze, telling himself that he was simply seeing some strange type of lightning, or perhaps a hallucination brought on by the cold, but the light dipped out of view for a moment before returning. Hallucination or not, he realized after a few seconds that he could see a boat, and that somehow – impossibly – it was making its way closer. He told himself that there was no way he could possibly be rescued, and he tried to rid his mind of what he assumed must be false hope, but the light was still approaching and he finally spotted a dark shape getting tossed about on the waves. He blinked a couple of times as more rain crashed down all around, but he was starting to think that maybe – just maybe – he was going to be rescued.

Or was it just another ghost ship?

Remembering all the spectral vessels that he'd seen earlier, just before he'd been dragged beneath the surface of the sandbank, he realized that another ghostly vision might be giving him false hope. As the boat edged closer, however, he realized that it looked fairly modern, that in fact it wasn't very different from the boats that usually stood along the shore at Crowford. He still couldn't quite believe that a miracle was about to happen, but he was starting to at least believe in the possibility.

"You there!" a voice shouted suddenly, barely making itself heard over the sound of the crashing waves. "We're coming around! Grab the rope!"

He saw a hand waving at him, and he immediately began to push through the waves, trying to get to the boat before he got washed away. He was quickly knocked off his feet, but he managed to start swimming, and a moment later he saw that a rope had been thrown over the boat's side. He tried to get to the rope, only for a wave to knock him to the side. Every muscle in his body was burning with pain, but he knew that this was his last chance to get to safety, so he swam furiously toward the rope and after a few more failed attempts he finally managed to grab hold.

"We're going to pull you up!" the voice yelled.

Gripping the rope as tight as he could with both hands, Johnny was tossed about in the waves as he felt the rope being pulled back up toward the deck of the boat. Soon as he right down by the boat's side, and a moment later he began to climb. Emerging from the water, he hauled himself up, but then he froze again as he saw the name of the boat painted on its side. He told himself he was wrong, that there must be a mistake, but for a few seconds he could only stare at the name in horror.

The *Mercy Belle*.

"Come on!" the voice called out. "You can do it!"

Looking up, Johnny realized he was almost onboard. A hand was reaching out to him, but for a moment he could only stare at the man who was trying to help him. Percy Weaver, one of the three men who'd died five years ago on the *Mercy Belle*, reached a little further but still couldn't quite get close enough.

"Hurry!" Percy shouted, as the boat tipped again against the waves. "We don't have much time!"

CHAPTER TWENTY-NINE

GRIPPING PERCY'S HAND TIGHT, Johnny finally scrambled onto the deck and fell down, slipping on the soaking wood. Rain was still falling all around, and another flash of lightning briefly lit up the boat as Johnny looked over toward the compartment where the captain was already frantically turning the wheel.

"Lund," Johnny whispered incredulously. "Captain John Lund."

"It's a miracle we saw you!" Percy yelled as he helped Johnny to his feet. "This storm came on so fast, we almost turned back and went over to Calais, but the captain said we could make it home. Now I'm not so sure."

Johnny turned to him.

"I don't mind telling you," Percy continued,

"it wasn't a unanimous decision to come and rescue you. Keith argued that we'd be going too far out of our way, and that it was too dangerous to go so close to the sands in this weather, but old Lund insisted he could do it. I guess we should never have doubted him. Still, I'm starting to think that Keith was right. We might not make it back to Crowford now, but it's too late for Calais. We just have to pray to the Lord that we make it."

Before Johnny could say a word, the boat was hit by another huge wave. Slamming against the railing, Johnny let out a gasp as he felt a sharp pain in his side.

"What are you doing out here, anyway?" Percy asked. "Are you alone? Where's your boat?"

"I don't get it," Johnny replied, as he saw Keith Simmons working on one of the other ropes. "How is this happening? Why did you bring me out here, only to rescue me?"

"Why did we *what*?" Percy asked.

Johnny turned to him, and in that moment he realized that Percy no longer looked dead. It was as if, somehow, he'd been restored to life.

"Lund," Johnny whispered. "I have to talk to Lund."

Turning, he gripped the railing as he struggled over to the fishing boat's cabin. Wave after wave was crashing against the boat's side, but somehow Johnny managed to stay on his feet. His mind was racing and he was still trying to work out how he'd ended up on the *Mercy Belle*, and how a ghost ship could feel so real. After all, he knew without a shadow of doubt that the Mercy Belle had been destroyed five years earlier.

"Johnny Eggars, is that you?" Captain Lund yelled as soon as he reached the cabin. "What the hell are you doing here?"

"Are you insane?" Percy shouted behind him. "You could have been killed!"

"I..."

Staring at Captain Lund, Johnny was still frantically trying to understand what was happening. He stood frozen for a moment as the boat almost tipped again, but the sight of these dead men was almost too much for him to comprehend. When they'd appeared as ghosts, he'd at least understood what was happening, even if he'd struggled to believe that it was real; now they looked to be alive, and somehow that was even more confusing.

"We should never have turned around for you," Percy shouted. "This storm's getting stronger by the second. We'll never make it home!"

"You've doomed us!" Keith Simmons called out from the far end of the deck. "We'll never see the shore again, and it's all your fault!"

"No," Johnny whispered, "I didn't... I don't..."

"Everyone get back to your stations!" Captain Lund yelled. "We're not giving up yet, not without a fight! I want you all to do your jobs! And as for you -"

He turned to Johnny.

"I don't know how in God's name you ended up here," he continued, "but you might as well at least be useful. Get in here and help me secure the wheel!"

Stepping into the cabin, Johnny grabbed the wheel. The two men tried to turn it together, but the waves were too strong and they were barely able to get the wheel to move at all.

"I called for help," Captain Lund said, "but I don't know that anyone'll make it out to us. I'm not even sure that I'd want them to, not in this weather. There's no point in any more lives being put at risk."

"I'm sorry," Johnny said. "Please, you have to believe me, I don't understand what's happening."

"A likely story," Captain Lund replied. "When we get to dry land, man, you'll have some explaining to do, starting with -"

Suddenly Keith cried out. Johnny turned and looked out at the deck, just in time to see Keith being carried over the side by a huge wave. The man's scream was quickly lost in the roar of the storm, and a moment later another wave crashed against the boat's other side, causing a sickening cracking sound that could only mean that the hull was damaged.

"Grab him!" Captain Lund shouted, even though Keith was already gone.

"I don't see him!" Percy shouted, rushing over to the railing and looking out at the sea in a desperate attempt to spot the lost man. "Keith! Can you hear me?"

"No man could survive being down there," Captain Lund muttered. "We've lost him. May the Lord have mercy on his soul, and may his family -"

Another huge wave crashed against the side of the boat. Johnny saw Percy getting tossed across the deck and slamming against one of the railings. He saw the man's head being torn from his shoulders, and then Percy too was gone, washed over the side and taken by the sea. At the same time, the entire boat was creaking now, and Johnny realized that the hull was well and truly broken.

"She's lost," Captain Lund said, stepping back from the wheel. "There's no hope now."

"That's not true!" Johnny replied, grabbing the wheel but quickly realizing that there was nothing he could do. "We can't give up now!"

"I'll never see my Moira again," Captain Lund continued. "Or my sons, either. I only hope that they know I loved them, and that I fought to the last to save my vessel. If only I could see them one final time and tell them how much they -"

Before he could finish, another huge wave crashed against the side of the boat, obliterating the cabin and tossing Johnny and Captain Lund out into the raging sea. As he slammed into the water, Edward heard Captain Lund cry out one final time, and then he turned and saw a large piece of wood landing nearby. Grabbing the wood and clinging on for dear life, he looked around in the vain hope of spotting the captain, but there was no sign of the other man anywhere. Another wave hit Johnny, almost knocking him off the wood, but he somehow held on. Shivering in the rain, he gripped the wood tighter, but then yet another wave lifted him up before sending him crashing down.

He turned to again look for Captain Lund, but at that moment the storm whipped up another chunk of wood and sent it crashing against Johnny's face. He screamed as he felt the wood's sharp edge cutting across his face, and for a moment the chunk was embedded deep in his flesh. He managed to push the wood away, but seconds later a wave battered him again, and this time something struck him hard on the back of the head, with such force that he was almost knocked out.

Bloodied and bleeding, he clung to the piece of wood and waited for death. He could feel the blood flowing from his wounds, and at the same time he could also feel his mind starting to fade. He realized after a moment that he could no longer quite remember how he'd ended up out at sea. Trying not to panic, he focused hard, and at first he didn't notice the flashing light that was starting to pick him out. Instead, he was desperately trying to keep hold of the memories that – even now – were draining away from his thoughts.

Somewhere nearby, a voice was shouting out at him, but he wasn't strong enough to listen. Instead, he could feel himself forgetting everything about his old life, as if the memories were being washed away with the blood that was pouring from his wounds. And then, suddenly, he felt a hand on his shoulder.

Startled, he turned and saw that a man had joined him on the piece of wood. The man was attached to a rope, and the rope was attached to a lifeboat. For a moment, Johnny felt sure that he recognized the lifeboat, and that he recognized the man too, but the last hint of those memories quickly slipped away and he realized that he didn't even know his own name. He remembered absolutely nothing.

"It's going to be okay," the man said breathlessly, as the storm continued to toss them in the storm. "My name's Johnny. Johnny Eggars. We're going to get you out of here."

CHAPTER THIRTY

Five years later...

KNEELING ON THE BEACH, down at the shore, Edward Smith stared out at the calm water and realized that his name wasn't Edward Smith at all. His eyes – all that remained of a face that had been destroyed in the storm five years earlier – blinked a couple of times, and he felt as if the block in his mind had suddenly disappeared.

He remembered everything.

"Darling?" Hazel said cautiously, limping over to join him. "Are you..."

He turned to her.

She hesitated, before kneeling next to him. For a moment, they both remained silent, as if neither of them could quite comprehend everything that had just happened. Manners lay dead nearby, and the flare gun lay helplessly on the shingles. A couple of minutes had now passed since the little wooden boat had disappeared into the darkness out at sea, carrying Johnny – the other, younger Johnny – away.

"You remember now, don't you?" Hazel said cautiously. "Tell me you remember."

"Johnny," he whispered. "I'm Johnny Eggars."

She stared at him, and then slowly she nodded.

"You..." He paused. "You knew?"

"I didn't *know*," she replied. "I suspected, though. I don't know how, but the moment I first saw you five years ago, despite your awful injuries, I had a feeling. It didn't make sense, of course, because you were also standing right next to me, and I didn't understand how both of you could be the same man. But as I helped you recover, I felt more and more sure that it was somehow true. I couldn't say anything, though. Nobody would have believed me. I just... waited, to see what would happen."

"But it's 1955, right?" he asked.

She nodded again.

He turned and looked out to sea, and he remembered the terror he'd felt when he'd been taken out there by the ghosts of the *Mercy Belle*'s crew. He realized that the younger version of himself was out there now, and was about to get dragged down into the sand, and then...

And then what?

Then he'd get spat back out, except suddenly he'd have traveled back five years into the past. That was impossible, yet it had somehow happened. He thought back to the day when Willy had been dragged under the surface of the sandbank, only to get spat back out several feet away, and he realized that something similar must have happened again. Except this time, instead of spitting him out in a different location, the sand had somehow sent him out in a different year.

"We have to call for help," Hazel said. "Johnny, I mean the other you, is out there, he -"

"No," Johnny said.

"No?"

"No." He paused, still thinking back to that awful night. "I think he has to go. He always did. But it's okay, because the sand will forgive him. It'll even give him another chance, although..." He reached up and touched his ravaged face. "Although he won't know it at first," he added. "I guess he couldn't be allowed to remember, not while there were two of him in one town. Two of *me*."

"But how did this happen?" Hazel asked, as she slowly got to her feet. "I still don't understand, did he somehow..."

She looked out at the dark, calm sea. Even now, she couldn't help thinking about the sight of Johnny – the other Johnny, the Johnny from before the wreck of the *Mercy Belle* – being taken away by the ghostly figures of three dead men.

"Did he somehow go back five years?" she asked finally. "How... I mean... How is something like that ever possible?"

"I don't think we'll ever really understand," he replied. "Maybe at the end, the sands decided that I should get another chance." He turned to her. "All I know is that I'm here, and I finally remember everything that happened. I'll try to explain it to you, at least the part that I can figure out, but the rest of it is just going to be something of a blur. I'll do my best, though." He reached out and took her hand, and he let her help him up. "I guess that's all we *can* do."

***

Standing in the spare bedroom, Johnny stared down at Tobias.

His son.

His son.

Some parts of his new life were going to be easier to get to grips with than others. He remembered the entirety of the five years he'd spent as Edward Smith, and he now remembered all his life before that, but he was still having trouble reconciling those two periods. He tried to tell himself that eventually he'd figure it out, although in truth he wasn't quite sure whether that would happen. He figured that, instead, he might have to simply accept that some parts of his story would never fit together neatly, and that he'd never truly understand why the sands had done what they'd done.

At least, however, he was getting a second chance.

Reaching into the crib, he carefully lifted Tobias up. His son let out a happy gurgle, and Johnny held him in his arms and stared down at his face.

"Hey," he said, and he could hear his voice trembling a little, "it's all okay. Daddy's here. I guess, as far as you're concerned, Daddy's *always* been here. I've got to tell you, though, things have been a little complicated for Mummy and me. That's going to change, though. From now on, we're going to be living without that shadow hanging over us. Now we know that we have a future. I don't know if you ever sensed that something wasn't quite right, but that's all over now, I promise."

Hearing footsteps, he turned to see that Hazel was entering the room, carrying two hot cups of tea.

"So you really knew it was me all along,

huh?" he said, as she set the cups down. "I can't imagine how it must have been for you, living like that for five years and keeping the truth to yourself."

"Do you think I should have told you?"

He thought about that question for a moment.

"No," he said finally. "I don't think so. Or the other me. I doubt we really would have believed you."

"You'd both have thought that I was crazy. I half expected someone else to have some suspicions, maybe Harry or Willy, but somehow it slipped right by them. I suppose it's not really something that would ever occur to most people. Plus, you look so different, and even your voice was changed a little by your injuries."

"Thank you, though," he continued. "Without you, I..."

His voice trailed off.

"I love you," she told him, as she put a hand on the side of his arm. "I always have. When I realized that somehow it was you who'd survived the wreck of the *Mercy Belle*, at first I tried to figure it all out, but I couldn't. So I did the only thing that I *could* do, I stuck by you and I cared for you and I helped you. I suppose I knew that one day the truth would come out, and I just got on with things and waited for that day to arrive." She paused. "And now here it is."

"Here it is," he said, echoing her as he looked back down at Tobias.

"You must have been so terrified when you were dragged out there by Captain Lund and the others," she continued. "I saw the look on your face, you were so confused. It was at that moment, though, that I started to see how the two versions of you might start to make sense. Still, I always knew that the sands were mysterious and dangerous, but I never thought they could actually do something like this. I guess there's a very good reason why sailors have always given them a wide berth. Not just because of the risk of getting shipwrecked, but also because..."

"I don't think there's ever been anyone who understands the sands," he told her, "and we don't need to, not really. We just need to know that we shouldn't interfere, and we need to resist the temptation to go out there and look for answers."

Tobias gurgled again.

"I think," Johnny added, "that we're going to be pretty busy raising this little one. And any others who come along."

He set Tobias back down in the crib and turned to his wife.

"I'm sorry you had to go through so much," he told her. "I'm sorry that, at times over the past five years, I've caused so much trouble. But I'm here now, and I promise you, I won't ever go anywhere again."

"You'd better not," she said, stepping closer and looking into his eyes, before leaning toward him for a kiss. "Not now that I've finally got you back."

EPILOGUE 1

One year later...

"I JUST WANTED TO tell you that I thought your little speech at the memorial service last night was beautiful," Mrs. Carter told Johnny as they stood in the street. "I must admit, Mr. Smith, it's a huge relief for everyone to finally know what happened before the *Mercy Belle* was destroyed. I feel as if a huge weight has been lifted off the entire town."

"I'm only sorry that it took me so long to remember," he replied.

"I spoke to one of Captain Lund's sons last night," she continued. "He told me that his mother was very moved to hear the truth. It's really put her mind at rest."

"I went and spoke to Moira a few days ago,"

he explained. "And to the families of Mr. Weaver and Mr. Simmons, too. I thought they should hear it from me, before I spoke about it at the ceremony."

Before Mrs. Carter could reply, the bell rang above the door of a nearby shop, and she turned to see that Hazel was carrying Tobias out to join them.

"And how is this little fellow handling being a big brother?" Mrs. Carter asked, before looking down into the pram and smiling at the newborn baby. "What's her name, again?"

"Angela," Johnny said, as he watched his daughter staring up at him. "Tobias is doing just fine as a big brother. I've got a feeling he'll always be there to look after her. No matter what."

As Mrs. Carter started talking to Hazel about the new baby, Johnny couldn't help looking along the street and watching the people of Crowford going about their business. His speech the previous night, at the ceremony to mark the sixth anniversary of the *Mercy Belle* tragedy, genuinely seemed to have brought about a change in the town. He hadn't been able to tell people the whole truth, of course; after all, how could he possibly have expected them to believe a story that involved him getting sent back in time five years by the sands? He hadn't even been able to reveal his true identity, but he supposed that continuing to live as Edward Smith wasn't too harsh a price to pay for the fact that he was continuing to live at all.

As far as the people of Crowford were concerned, Johnny Eggars had simply disappeared one night at sea, and had most likely drowned. His parents had died several years earlier, and he'd been living with his uncle, who knew the sea well enough to understand that Johnny was most likely dead. The circumstances of his death had been vague, but a small gravestone had been erected in the cemetery. A few months later, Johnny's uncle had died of a heart attack.

Spotting some familiar faces, Johnny watched as Willy and Harry wandered past on their way to yet another pub. Sometimes he missed hanging out with them, but he knew it would be too risky to try to befriend them again. Besides, he was a family man now, and he didn't really have time to sit around drinking. He briefly made eye contact with his two old friends, and they exchanged a nod, but he was confident that they had no clue as to his true identity. And that was how things were going to have to stay.

"Got to dash," Mrs. Carter said suddenly, jolting Johnny back into the conversation. He turned to see that she was waving as she walked away. "If I don't see you before, just drop Tobias and Angela over around six tonight. I can't wait to spend a couple of hours with them."

"She's babysitting for us?" Johnny said, turning to Hazel. "Tonight? Why?"

"We're getting out of the house," she replied as they began to make their way along the street, heading home.

"Where are we going?"

"Well, don't take this the wrong way," she said cautiously, "but there are some dance classes at the town hall every Thursday evening, and I thought it's still not too late to see if we can lick you into shape. And before you say another word, that bad leg of yours isn't going to be a valid excuse."

As they walked away, discussing the class and Johnny's supposed dance skills, they walked past a crowd that had gathered to witness the reopening of the pier. All the structural repairs had been made, and this time the surveyors were confident that there'd be no more problems. A few people were already starting to make their way along the pier, which stretched out from the shore, reaching roughly a thousand feet across the calm, blue water that lay glittering beneath the afternoon sun.

Further out still, the sands lay baking in the heat. Tiny shrimp were going about their lives in the shallow pools of water that dotted the sands, while the sands themselves showed no scars from any of the activities that had recently taken place on their surface. As always, the grains had quickly covered up any disturbance. The sands simply lay in the sun, watching and waiting, guardians of an unspoken, unwritten contract between the land and the sea.

EPILOGUE 2

Today...

A short distance from the neglected gravestone of Johnny Eggars, another stone stood next to the path that ran through the cemetery. This stone, although it had been abandoned along with all the rest, had at least been tended for many years while the town was still inhabited. This was a stone where people had stopped to mark their respects, and where flowers had for many years been left on birthdays. It was a stone that meant something to people in Crowford. Although it was simple, this stone had been chosen with great care and love. The stone marked the burial spot of two people whose bodies lay down in the ground, in adjacent coffins, and who had lived long and happy lives together:

In memory of

Edward Smith
d. 18th March 1998

and his wife

Hazel Smith
nee Christie
b. 23rd July 1926
d. 20th September 1998

Beloved parents and grandparents

Coming Soon

THE GHOST OF CROWFORD SCHOOL

The year is 1989. As their final term at Crowford Primary School draws to an end, five friends realize that they might never have another chance to investigate the town's darkest mystery. Does a ghostly figure really haunt the old school building?

Determined to discover the truth, the friends come up with a plan. The old school has stood empty and untouched for several decades, but rumors persist of a terrifying vision that awaits anyone who goes inside. As they force their way into the school's abandoned rooms, the five kids are convinced that they're going to get a glimpse of the evil that lurks within. Instead, they find something that might never let them leave again...

Also available

THE HAUNTING OF NELSON STREET

Crowford, a sleepy coastal town in the south of England, might seem like an oasis of calm and tranquility. Beneath the surface, however, dark secrets are waiting to claim fresh victims, and ghostly figures plot revenge.

Having finally decided to leave the hustle of London, Daisy and Richard Johnson buy two houses on Nelson Street, a picturesque street in the center of Crowford. One house is perfect and ready to move into, while the other is a fire-ravaged wreck that needs a lot of work.

Soon, they discover that the two houses share a common link to the past. Something awful once happened on Nelson Street, something that shook the town to its core. Before they can face Crowford's horrors, however, Daisy and Richard have to deal with the ghosts of their own recent history. What is Daisy hiding, and why does Richard feel strangely drawn to one of the town's strangest inhabitants?

AMY CROSS

Also by Amy Cross

The Devil, the Witch and the Whore
(The Deal book 1)

"Leave the forest alone. Whatever's out there, just let it be. Don't make it angry."

When a horrific discovery is made at the edge of town, Sheriff James Kopperud realizes the answers he seeks might be waiting beyond in the vast forest. But everybody in the town of Deal knows that there's something out there in the forest, something that should never be disturbed. A deal was made long ago, a deal that was supposed to keep the town safe. And if he insists on investigating the murder of a local girl, James is going to have to break that deal and head out into the wilderness.

Meanwhile, James has no idea that his estranged daughter Ramsey has returned to town. Ramsey is running from something, and she thinks she can find safety in the vast tunnel system that runs beneath the forest. Before long, however, Ramsey finds herself coming face to face with creatures that hide in the shadows. One of these creatures is known as the devil, and another is known as the witch. They're both waiting for the whore to arrive, but for very different reasons. And soon Ramsey is offered a terrible deal, one that could save or destroy the entire town, and maybe even the world.

AMY CROSS

Also by Amy Cross

The Soul Auction

"I saw a woman on the beach. I watched her face a demon."

Thirty years after her mother's death, Alice Ashcroft is drawn back to the coastal English town of Curridge. Somebody in Curridge has been reviewing Alice's novels online, and in those reviews there have been tantalizing hints at a hidden truth. A truth that seems to be linked to her dead mother.

"Thirty years ago, there was a soul auction."

Once she reaches Curridge, Alice finds strange things happening all around her. Something attacks her car. A figure watches her on the beach at night. And when she tries to find the person who has been reviewing her books, she makes a horrific discovery.

What really happened to Alice's mother thirty years ago? Who was she talking to, just moments before dropping dead on the beach? What caused a huge rockfall that nearly tore a nearby cliff-face in half? And what sinister presence is lurking in the grounds of the local church?

Also by Amy Cross

Darper Danver: The Complete First Series

Five years ago, three friends went to a remote cabin in the woods and tried to contact the spirit of a long-dead soldier. They thought they could control whatever happened next. They were wrong...

Newly released from prison, Cassie Briggs returns to Fort Powell, determined to get her life back on track. Soon, however, she begins to suspect that an ancient evil still lurks in the nearby cabin. Was the mysterious Darper Danver really destroyed all those years ago, or does her spirit still linger, waiting for a chance to return?

As Cassie and her ex-boyfriend Fisher are finally forced to face the truth about what happened in the cabin, they realize that Darper isn't ready to let go of their lives just yet. Meanwhile, a vengeful woman plots revenge for her brother's murder, and a New York ghost writer arrives in town to uncover the truth. Before long, strange carvings begin to appear around town and blood starts to flow once again.

Also by Amy Cross

The Ghost of Molly Holt

"Molly Holt is dead. There's nothing to fear in this house."

When three teenagers set out to explore an abandoned house in the middle of a forest, they think they've found the location where the infamous Molly Holt video was filmed.

They've found much more than that...

Tim doesn't believe in ghosts, but he has a crush on a girl who does. That's why he ends up taking her out to the house, and it's also why he lets her take his only flashlight. But as they explore the house together, Tim and Becky start to realize that something else might be lurking in the shadows.

Something that, ten years ago, suffered unimaginable pain.

Something that won't rest until a terrible wrong has been put right.

Also by Amy Cross

American Coven

He kidnapped three women and held them in his basement. He thought they couldn't fight back. He was wrong...

Snatched from the street near her home, Holly Carter is taken to a rural house and thrown down into a stone basement. She meets two other women who have also been kidnapped, and soon Holly learns about the horrific rituals that take place in the house. Eventually, she's called upstairs to take her place in the ice bath.

As her nightmare continues, however, Holly learns about a mysterious power that exists in the basement, and which the three women might be able to harness. When they finally manage to get through the metal door, however, the women have no idea that their fight for freedom is going to stretch out for more than a decade, or that it will culminate in a final, devastating demonstration of their new-found powers.

Also by Amy Cross

The Ash House

Why would anyone ever return to a haunted house?

For Diane Mercer the answer is simple. She's dying of cancer, and she wants to know once and for all whether ghosts are real.

Heading home with her young son, Diane is determined to find out whether the stories are real. After all, everyone else claimed to see and hear strange things in the house over the years. Everyone except Diane had some kind of experience in the house, or in the little ash house in the yard.

As Diane explores the house where she grew up, however, her son is exploring the yard and the forest. And while his mother might be struggling to come to terms with her own impending death, Daniel Mercer is puzzled by fleeting appearances of a strange little girl who seems drawn to the ash house, and by strange, rasping coughs that he keeps hearing at night.

The Ash House is a horror novel about a woman who desperately wants to know what will happen to her when she dies, and about a boy who uncovers the shocking truth about a young girl's murder.

Also by Amy Cross

Haunted

Twenty years ago, the ghost of a dead little girl drove Sheriff Michael Blaine to his death.

Now, that same ghost is coming for his daughter.

Returning to the small town where she grew up, Alex Roberts is determined to live a normal, quiet life. For the residents of Railham, however, she's an unwelcome reminder of the town's darkest hour.

Twenty years ago, nine-year-old Mo Garvey was found brutally murdered in a nearby forest. Everyone thinks that Alex's father was responsible, but if the killer was brought to justice, why is the ghost of Mo Garvey still after revenge?

And how far will the real killer go to protect his secret, when Alex starts getting closer to the truth?

Haunted is a horror novel about a woman who has to face her past, about a town that would rather forget, and about a little girl who refuses to let death stand in her way.

AMY CROSS

Also by Amy Cross

The Curse of Wetherley House

"If you walk through that door, Evil Mary will get you."

When she agrees to visit a supposedly haunted house with an old friend, Rosie assumes she'll encounter nothing more scary than a few creaks and bumps in the night. Even the legend of Evil Mary doesn't put her off. After all, she knows ghosts aren't real. But when Mary makes her first appearance, Rosie realizes she might already be trapped.

For more than a century, Wetherley House has been cursed. A horrific encounter on a remote road in the late 1800's has already caused a chain of misery and pain for all those who live at the house. Wetherley House was abandoned long ago, after a terrible discovery in the basement, something has remained undetected within its room. And even the local children know that Evil Mary waits in the house for anyone foolish enough to walk through the front door.

Before long, Rosie realizes that her entire life has been defined by the spirit of a woman who died in agony. Can she become the first person to escape Evil Mary, or will she fall victim to the same fate as the house's other occupants?

AMY CROSS

Also by Amy Cross

The Ghosts of Hexley Airport

Ten years ago, more than two hundred people died in a horrific plane crash at Hexley Airport.

Today, some say their ghosts still haunt the terminal building.

When she starts her new job at the airport, working a night shift as part of the security team, Casey assumes the stories about the place can't be true. Even when she has a strange encounter in a deserted part of the departure hall, she's certain that ghosts aren't real.

Soon, however, she's forced to face the truth. Not only is there something haunting the airport's buildings and tarmac, but a sinister force is working behind the scenes to replicate the circumstances of the original accident. And as a snowstorm moves in, Hexley Airport looks set to witness yet another disaster.

AMY CROSS

Also by Amy Cross

The Girl Who Never Came Back

Twenty years ago, Charlotte Abernathy vanished while playing near her family's house. Despite a frantic search, no trace of her was found until a year later, when the little girl turned up on the doorstep with no memory of where she'd been.

Today, Charlotte has put her mysterious ordeal behind her, even though she's never learned where she was during that missing year. However, when her eight-year-old niece vanishes in similar circumstances, a fully-grown Charlotte is forced to make a fresh attempt to uncover the truth.

Originally published in 2013, the fully revised and updated version of *The Girl Who Never Came Back* tells the harrowing story of a woman who thought she could forget her past, and of a little girl caught in the tangled web of a dark family secret.

AMY CROSS

Also by Amy Cross

Asylum
(The Asylum Trilogy book 1)

"No-one ever leaves Lakehurst. The staff, the patients, the ghosts... Once you're here, you're stuck forever."

After shooting her little brother dead, Annie Radford is sent to Lakehurst psychiatric hospital for assessment. Hearing voices in her head, Annie is forced to undergo experimental new treatments devised by a mysterious old man who lives in the hospital's attic. It soon becomes clear that the hospital's staff, led by the vicious Nurse Winter, are hiding something horrific at Lakehurst.

As Annie struggles to survive the hospital, she learns more about Nurse Winter's own story. Once a promising young medical student, Kirsten Winter also heard voices in her head. Voices that traveled a long way to reach her. Voices that have a plan of their own. Voices that will stop at nothing to get what they want.

What kind of signals are being transmitted from the basement of the hospital? Who is the old man in the attic? Why are living human brains kept in jars? And what is the dark secret that lurks at the heart of the hospital?

AMY CROSS

BOOKS BY AMY CROSS

1. Dark Season: The Complete First Series (2011)
2. Werewolves of Soho (Lupine Howl book 1) (2012)
3. Werewolves of the Other London (Lupine Howl book 2) (2012)
4. Ghosts: The Complete Series (2012)
5. Dark Season: The Complete Second Series (2012)
6. The Children of Black Annis (Lupine Howl book 3) (2012)
7. Destiny of the Last Wolf (Lupine Howl book 4) (2012)
8. Asylum (The Asylum Trilogy book 1) (2012)
9. Dark Season: The Complete Third Series (2013)
10. Devil's Briar (2013)
11. Broken Blue (The Broken Trilogy book 1) (2013)
12. The Night Girl (2013)
13. Days 1 to 4 (Mass Extinction Event book 1) (2013)
14. Days 5 to 8 (Mass Extinction Event book 2) (2013)
15. The Library (The Library Chronicles book 1) (2013)
16. American Coven (2013)
17. Werewolves of Sangreth (Lupine Howl book 5) (2013)
18. Broken White (The Broken Trilogy book 2) (2013)
19. Grave Girl (Grave Girl book 1) (2013)
20. Other People's Bodies (2013)
21. The Shades (2013)
22. The Vampire's Grave and Other Stories (2013)
23. Darper Danver: The Complete First Series (2013)
24. The Hollow Church (2013)
25. The Dead and the Dying (2013)
26. Days 9 to 16 (Mass Extinction Event book 3) (2013)
27. The Girl Who Never Came Back (2013)
28. Ward Z (The Ward Z Series book 1) (2013)
29. Journey to the Library (The Library Chronicles book 2) (2014)
30. The Vampires of Tor Cliff Asylum (2014)
31. The Family Man (2014)
32. The Devil's Blade (2014)
33. The Immortal Wolf (Lupine Howl book 6) (2014)
34. The Dying Streets (Detective Laura Foster book 1) (2014)
35. The Stars My Home (2014)
36. The Ghost in the Rain and Other Stories (2014)
37. Ghosts of the River Thames (The Robinson Chronicles book 1) (2014)
38. The Wolves of Cur'eath (2014)
39. Days 46 to 53 (Mass Extinction Event book 4) (2014)
40. The Man Who Saw the Face of the World (2014)

AMY CROSS

41. The Art of Dying (Detective Laura Foster book 2) (2014)
42. Raven Revivals (Grave Girl book 2) (2014)
43. Arrival on Thaxos (Dead Souls book 1) (2014)
44. Birthright (Dead Souls book 2) (2014)
45. A Man of Ghosts (Dead Souls book 3) (2014)
46. The Haunting of Hardstone Jail (2014)
47. A Very Respectable Woman (2015)
48. Better the Devil (2015)
49. The Haunting of Marshall Heights (2015)
50. Terror at Camp Everbee (The Ward Z Series book 2) (2015)
51. Guided by Evil (Dead Souls book 4) (2015)
52. Child of a Bloodied Hand (Dead Souls book 5) (2015)
53. Promises of the Dead (Dead Souls book 6) (2015)
54. Days 54 to 61 (Mass Extinction Event book 5) (2015)
55. Angels in the Machine (The Robinson Chronicles book 2) (2015)
56. The Curse of Ah-Qal's Tomb (2015)
57. Broken Red (The Broken Trilogy book 3) (2015)
58. The Farm (2015)
59. Fallen Heroes (Detective Laura Foster book 3) (2015)
60. The Haunting of Emily Stone (2015)
61. Cursed Across Time (Dead Souls book 7) (2015)
62. Destiny of the Dead (Dead Souls book 8) (2015)
63. The Death of Jennifer Kazakos (Dead Souls book 9) (2015)
64. Alice Isn't Well (Death Herself book 1) (2015)
65. Annie's Room (2015)
66. The House on Everley Street (Death Herself book 2) (2015)
67. Meds (The Asylum Trilogy book 2) (2015)
68. Take Me to Church (2015)
69. Ascension (Demon's Grail book 1) (2015)
70. The Priest Hole (Nykolas Freeman book 1) (2015)
71. Eli's Town (2015)
72. The Horror of Raven's Briar Orphanage (Dead Souls book 10) (2015)
73. The Witch of Thaxos (Dead Souls book 11) (2015)
74. The Rise of Ashalla (Dead Souls book 12) (2015)
75. Evolution (Demon's Grail book 2) (2015)
76. The Island (The Island book 1) (2015)
77. The Lighthouse (2015)
78. The Cabin (The Cabin Trilogy book 1) (2015)
79. At the Edge of the Forest (2015)
80. The Devil's Hand (2015)
81. The 13th Demon (Demon's Grail book 3) (2016)
82. After the Cabin (The Cabin Trilogy book 2) (2016)
83. The Border: The Complete Series (2016)
84. The Dead Ones (Death Herself book 3) (2016)

85. A House in London (2016)
86. Persona (The Island book 2) (2016)
87. Battlefield (Nykolas Freeman book 2) (2016)
88. Perfect Little Monsters and Other Stories (2016)
89. The Ghost of Shapley Hall (2016)
90. The Blood House (2016)
91. The Death of Addie Gray (2016)
92. The Girl With Crooked Fangs (2016)
93. Last Wrong Turn (2016)
94. The Body at Auercliff (2016)
95. The Printer From Hell (2016)
96. The Dog (2016)
97. The Nurse (2016)
98. The Haunting of Blackwych Grange (2016)
99. Twisted Little Things and Other Stories (2016)
100. The Horror of Devil's Root Lake (2016)
101. The Disappearance of Katie Wren (2016)
102. B&B (2016)
103. The Bride of Ashbyrn House (2016)
104. The Devil, the Witch and the Whore (The Deal Trilogy book 1) (2016)
105. The Ghosts of Lakeforth Hotel (2016)
106. The Ghost of Longthorn Manor and Other Stories (2016)
107. Laura (2017)
108. The Murder at Skellin Cottage (Jo Mason book 1) (2017)
109. The Curse of Wetherley House (2017)
110. The Ghosts of Hexley Airport (2017)
111. The Return of Rachel Stone (Jo Mason book 2) (2017)
112. Haunted (2017)
113. The Vampire of Downing Street and Other Stories (2017)
114. The Ash House (2017)
115. The Ghost of Molly Holt (2017)
116. The Camera Man (2017)
117. The Soul Auction (2017)
118. The Abyss (The Island book 3) (2017)
119. Broken Window (The House of Jack the Ripper book 1) (2017)
120. In Darkness Dwell (The House of Jack the Ripper book 2) (2017)
121. Cradle to Grave (The House of Jack the Ripper book 3) (2017)
122. The Lady Screams (The House of Jack the Ripper book 4) (2017)
123. A Beast Well Tamed (The House of Jack the Ripper book 5) (2017)
124. Doctor Charles Grazier (The House of Jack the Ripper book 6) (2017)
125. The Raven Watcher (The House of Jack the Ripper book 7) (2017)
126. The Final Act (The House of Jack the Ripper book 8) (2017)
127. Stephen (2017)
128. The Spider (2017)

AMY CROSS

129. The Mermaid's Revenge (2017)
130. The Girl Who Threw Rocks at the Devil (2018)
131. Friend From the Internet (2018)
132. Beautiful Familiar (2018)
133. One Night at a Soul Auction (2018)
134. 16 Frames of the Devil's Face (2018)
135. The Haunting of Caldgrave House (2018)
136. Like Stones on a Crow's Back (The Deal Trilogy book 2) (2018)
137. Room 9 and Other Stories (2018)
138. The Gravest Girl of All (Grave Girl book 3) (2018)
139. Return to Thaxos (Dead Souls book 13) (2018)
140. The Madness of Annie Radford (The Asylum Trilogy book 3) (2018)
141. The Haunting of Briarwych Church (Briarwych book 1) (2018)
142. I Just Want You To Be Happy (2018)
143. Day 100 (Mass Extinction Event book 6) (2018)
144. The Horror of Briarwych Church (Briarwych book 2) (2018)
145. The Ghost of Briarwych Church (Briarwych book 3) (2018)
146. Lights Out (2019)
147. Apocalypse (The Ward Z Series book 3) (2019)
148. Days 101 to 108 (Mass Extinction Event book 7) (2019)
149. The Haunting of Daniel Bayliss (2019)
150. The Purchase (2019)
151. Harper's Hotel Ghost Girl (Death Herself book 4) (2019)
152. The Haunting of Aldburn House (2019)
153. Days 109 to 116 (Mass Extinction Event book 8) (2019)
154. Bad News (2019)
155. The Wedding of Rachel Blaine (2019)
156. Dark Little Wonders and Other Stories (2019)
157. The Music Man (2019)
158. The Vampire Falls (Three Nights of the Vampire book 1) (2019)
159. The Other Ann (2019)
160. The Butcher's Husband and Other Stories (2019)
161. The Haunting of Lannister Hall (2019)
162. The Vampire Burns (Three Nights of the Vampire book 2) (2019)
163. Days 195 to 202 (Mass Extinction Event book 9) (2019)
164. Escape From Hotel Necro (2019)
165. The Vampire Rises (Three Nights of the Vampire book 3) (2019)
166. Ten Chimes to Midnight: A Collection of Ghost Stories (2019)
167. The Strangler's Daughter (2019)
168. The Beast on the Tracks (2019)
169. The Haunting of the King's Head (2019)
170. I Married a Serial Killer (2019)
171. Your Inhuman Heart (2020)
172. Days 203 to 210 (Mass Extinction Event book 10) (2020)

173. The Ghosts of David Brook (2020)
174. Days 349 to 356 (Mass Extinction Event book 11) (2020)
175. The Horror at Criven Farm (2020)
176. Mary (2020)
177. The Middlewych Experiment (Chaos Gear Annie book 1) (2020)
178. Days 357 to 364 (Mass Extinction Event book 12) (2020)
179. Day 365: The Final Day (Mass Extinction Event book 13) (2020)
180. The Haunting of Hathaway House (2020)
181. Don't Let the Devil Know Your Name (2020)
182. The Legend of Rinth (2020)
183. The Ghost of Old Coal House (2020)
184. The Root (2020)
185. I'm Not a Zombie (2020)
186. The Ghost of Annie Close (2020)
187. The Disappearance of Lonnie James (2020)
188. The Curse of the Langfords (2020)
189. The Haunting of Nelson Street (2020)
190. Strange Little Horrors and Other Stories (2020)
191. The House Where She Died (2020)

AMY CROSS

For more information, visit:

www.blackwychbooks.com

AMY CROSS

Made in the USA
Monee, IL
21 November 2020